Maria turned to head inside for extra supplies—then she saw him.

Her breath hitched. Her step faltered. The tray wobbled in her grip.

No. It couldn't be.

But it was.

"Ohmygod," her friend Trix murmured close behind her, "isn't that—"

"Yes," Maria said through clenched teeth. "Yes, it is."

She watched, frozen in a strange mix of fascination and dread, as Montgomery clasped the man she'd sworn she would never see again in a backslapping embrace.

"Now you're really going to have to tell me what happened," Trix said as soon as they were inside.

Maria slid the tray onto the counter behind the bar and shook off her trembling fingers. "What's he doing here, Trix?"

"Damned if I know. He's never been on board before. We'd best get the other stateroom made up."

"Oh, God, right. Yeah."

He'd be sleeping on board. For days. For nights.

She'd thought the yacht huge before. Now it was nowhere near big enough!

To set sail with the man she had slept with not one week ago...to wait on the man she had slept with...

Dear Reader,

I wholeheartedly believe in the "thunderbolt" Tim talks about in this story. Whether you call it insta-love or insta-lust, it's real. It happened with my husband, and twenty years down the line, I still feel the echoes of it.

But what happens when you've experienced that kind of love, only for life to cruelly take it away too soon? Do you believe it's a onetime-only deal? Tim certainly does. After losing his wife, his world becomes all about his daughter and his work. At forty-eight, love isn't just off his radar—it doesn't even seem possible.

Writing his second chance with a woman who's never known healthy romantic love was deeply rewarding. Watching that thunderbolt strike again, seeing him open his heart and convince Maria to trust hers, was magic. Because, in the end, it wasn't just Maria learning to love—it was Tim realizing that loving Maria didn't diminish what came before. And that he could indeed find joy in his past while fully embracing the future once more.

So here's to thunderbolts and the healing power of second chances—may you enjoy every moment with them!

Rachael x

CINDERELLA'S FLING WITH THE BILLIONAIRE

RACHAEL STEWART

Harlequin
ROMANCE

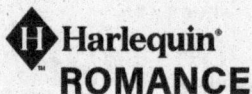

Harlequin® ROMANCE

ISBN-13: 978-1-335-47057-7

Cinderella's Fling with the Billionaire

For questions and comments about the quality of this book, please contact us at CustomerService@Harlequin.com.

TM and ® are trademarks of Harlequin Enterprises ULC.

Harlequin Enterprises ULC
22 Adelaide St. West, 41st Floor
Toronto, Ontario M5H 4E3, Canada
www.Harlequin.com

HarperCollins Publishers
Macken House, 39/40 Mayor Street Upper,
Dublin 1, D01 C9W8, Ireland
www.HarperCollins.com

Printed in U.S.A.

Recycling programs for this product may not exist in your area.

Rachael Stewart adores conjuring up stories, from heartwarmingly romantic to wildly erotic. She's been writing since she could put pen to paper—as the stacks of scrawled-on pages in her loft will attest to. A Welsh lass at heart, she now lives in Yorkshire, with her very own hero and three awesome kids—and if she's not tapping out a story, she's wrapped up in one or enjoying the great outdoors. Reach her on Facebook, X (@rach_b52) or at rachaelstewartauthor.com.

Visit the Author Profile page at Harlequin.com.

For Daphne,

Thank you for showing Dad the true wonder of Australia,

He's one lucky guy to have you in his life!

xxx

Praise for
Rachael Stewart

"This is a delightful, moving, contemporary romance....
I should warn you that this is the sort of book that once
you start you want to keep turning the pages until
you've read it. It is an enthralling story to escape into
and one that I thoroughly enjoyed reading.
I have no hesitation in highly recommending it."
—*Goodreads* on *Tempted by the Tycoon's Proposal*

CHAPTER ONE

TIMOTHY CAMPBELL SCANNED the grand ballroom of the Ritz-Carlton, the incessant rumble of Melbourne's elite an irritating buzz in his ear. Didn't matter that they were all here for him, his company and their latest win, every vibration mocked him and his lack of cheer.

A waiter approached, offering out a tray of champagne, and he waved him away.

He didn't want more alcohol.

He didn't want more small talk.

What he wanted was an escape.

'Great evening, Campbell.' Connor, his biggest investor and closest friend sidled up, a whisky in hand, his blond hair looking like he'd just rolled out of bed. His overbright blue eyes and flushed cheeks suggesting he hadn't been alone in the tumble either.

'The champagne not good enough for you?' he murmured.

'Not when you have a fifty-year-old Macallan

behind the bar.' Connor raised the crystal tumbler in salute. 'Thanks, by the way.'

'It comes out of your pocket too.'

'Damn, I forgot that bit.'

'Sure, you did.'

'Great party though, can always rely on you to throw the best.'

'Can always rely on you to lower the tone too.'

He gestured to his friend's slackened tie and unbuttoned collar. 'Who was it this time?'

Connor raised a lazy brow.

'Don't want to tell me?'

'Do you really want to know?'

He huffed. Connor had him there.

'What does it matter how we look anyway? No one cares when you make as much money as we do.'

'*You* should care.'

But then Connor wasn't a father. Hadn't been a husband. Hadn't felt the responsibility of wanting to be the best you could possibly be for those you loved.

And at forty-eight, Tim was in the best shape of his life. Physically. Financially. But mentally…

'You up for sailing next week? I'm taking the yacht out to Gabo…'

'Gabo?' Hell, Tim hadn't been there since… 'Maybe.'

'Maybe?' Connor raised the other brow. 'It appeals that much, hey?'

It did appeal—the open water, the fresh air, the freedom—but the memories…

'If we hadn't been friends for years, I'd be insulted at the face you're pulling.'

'And if I hadn't known you for years, I'd think there was a real risk of you being insulted.'

Connor laughed. 'My God, you need to get laid.'

'Getting laid,' he ground out, 'is the last thing I need.'

'Okay, laid is too crude.' Though he grinned as he said it. 'What I mean is, you need the love of a good woman to turn that frown upside down.'

'*Seriously*?'

'What?' Connor said, wide-eyed innocence all the way.

Did his friend really need reminding that the love of a good woman had been the instigator of said frown—the love and its loss?

'You're acting like I suggested you take a running leap off the nearest skyscraper.'

'You might as well have.'

'It's been seven years, buddy.' Concern softened Connor's tone, his eyes too, and Tim turned away—he couldn't bear that look.

'And it'll be another seven and I'll still stand here alone.'

'Why?'

'*Why?*' Tim snapped back around. 'Are you for real?'

'Yes! Is it guilt? Are you worried about Ellie turning over in her grave? Or are you worried about Sasha, because last I checked, Sasha was nagging *you* to date?'

'Coming from my daughter I'll take the nagging, but from you, the biggest player I know…?'

'Hey, before Ellie, *you* were the biggest player, or have you forgotten those days?'

No, he hadn't forgotten, but he'd been a different man then. He'd been younger for a start. Zero responsibility and all the drive to succeed.

'You worked hard, but you played harder. You had the best of both worlds.'

'How many times you been in love, Connor?'

'Alright, don't rub it in. We can't all be as lucky in love as you.'

He grunted. Lucky?

He'd *been* lucky, for sure. *So* lucky. He'd met Ellie at twenty-two, fallen in love and had Sasha within a year. His mates had thought he was crazy, tying himself down so young, but they were his motivation, his reason to succeed. And he had. His tech startup had made him one of the world's youngest self-made billionaires by the age of thirty.

For a long time, life had been perfect.

But luck came with its own expiry and his had run out. Seven years, one month and two days ago…or eight years if you counted the day that

Ellie's oncologist had delivered his blow. A terminal diagnosis with a grim prognosis.

And no amount of money had been able to save her—*them*—from that.

'You might try dating women your own age for a start,' he muttered, tugging himself out of the gloom to focus on Connor. Far easier to beat on his mate than himself.

'Ha! Can I help it if women half our age take a shine to me?' He nudged his head in the direction of the bar, where two young women were brazenly checking them out.

'You're old enough to be their father.'

'*And?* It's the experience they're after. Boys their age don't have a clue what they're doing.'

'And you think you do?'

'Ouch.' He palmed his chest. 'You really are on one tonight.'

'Sorry.' Tim ran a hand through his hair, blew out a breath. 'I'm just…'

'You're just in a melancholic spin. I know, I get it, I'm used to it. We're *all* used to it. But don't you think it's time you found a way out of it, before it's all you know too?'

His words chimed so readily with what Sasha had been saying on repeat for the past few years that he couldn't take it any more—time to bail.

'Campbell?' Connor hurried after him as he made for the exit. 'Where are you going?'

'Anywhere but here,' he said, his smile fixed in

place for the guests as he wove through the crowd, his speed making clear he wasn't for stopping.

'But it's still early and, if I'm not mistaken, those two look very much in need—'

'If you say getting laid again, I swear to God...'

Connor held up his hands. 'I was actually going to say *scintillating conversation.*'

'Of course you were.'

Connor's grin didn't waver. 'So, sailing next week, yeah?'

'You know your yacht has no sails, so technically it's not—'

'All right Mr Pedantic, just answer the question—you coming?'

'I'll think about it.'

'You need to stop thinking so hard because those wrinkles...' he drew a circle around his face '...they're only going to get worse.'

'Cheers for the tip,' Tim said with a slow, exaggerated nod. 'Now goodbye, Connor.'

And then he exited the room. It would be of no surprise to anyone that he'd scarpered without a formal farewell. He had form.

Initially, it had been a way to avoid the look in people's eyes, the pity. Then he'd lost patience with the platitudes and the meaningless conversation. Always eager to move on to the next thing that promised to occupy his mind and prevent it from turning to the past, to the pain, to Ellie.

Work and Sasha. They were his focus. But work no longer fulfilled him and Sasha—hell, Sasha was twenty-five and living her own life how she saw fit. She didn't need him any more.

And Tim… Tim had no idea what he needed, but it wasn't this.

Maria Thompson wiped down the bar and scanned the clientele.

To her mind, customers could be grouped into three camps:

Those who came for the company.

Those who came for solitude in said company.

And those who came looking for trouble, whatever form it took.

Tonight, Mickey's Bar rocked all three and her feet had barely touched the ground all evening.

'Hey, Mom.' Her eighteen-year-old daughter Fae set a tray of empties on the bar and stretched, arching her back with a groan that Maria felt all the way to her aching toes. 'Can I get another schooner for table four?'

'Already?' Maria frowned over at the guy. She'd served him not ten minutes ago and put him in the seeking solitude camp, but it was oh-so easy to slide into trouble with a few too many bevvies.

'Says he's had a day.'

He caught Maria's gaze and she gave a brief smile.

'Haven't we all…' she murmured, pouring him

a fresh one as she looked back at Fae, concern deepening as she took in her daughter's pallor, the dark shadows under her eyes... Not that the hair dye helped, the jet-black tone washing her daughter out so completely. But they'd been pulling long shifts lately, covering for two sick bar staff and another on holiday, and though it was great for the savings, it was clearly taking its toll.

'Why don't you get off? We'll be closing soon enough and Trix and I can cope until then.'

Trix was Mickey's niece and Maria's closest friend. Usually serving onboard superyachts, Trix was between charters and had stepped in as a favour to her uncle, giving up on her downtime to help them out.

'Nah,' Fae said, stifling a yawn. 'I'm good.'

'You're not good, you look ready to drop.'

'Gee, thanks.'

'It's meant in the nicest possible way. You've been working late all week, and were up early this morning to chip in with the cleaning.'

'So were you.'

'And I'm your mother. Now go. And make sure you eat! There's a slice of leftover lasagne in the fridge with your name on it.'

'What are you going to have?'

'Bob will see me right.' Bob was Mickey's chef, a giant of a man who scowled more than he smiled but had the biggest heart. He was also their neighbour in the flat above the bar. 'There's sure to be something left over after tonight's shift.'

And failing that she'd grab a bag of chips on her way up. Easy-peasy.

'Okay, but call me down if you get a sudden rush on.' She sent a hesitant glance in the direction of table four. 'And—'

'Watch him, I know. Don't forget, I taught you all that you know.'

Fae smiled and heaved herself over the bar to plant a kiss on her cheek. 'I learnt from the best.'

Maria smiled tightly. If best meant learning from someone who'd been through the worst courtesy of the opposite sex, then yup, that was her. 'Sweet dreams, honey.'

''Night, Mum. 'Night, Trix!' she hollered.

Trix looked up from clearing table six, her brown skin radiant, her eyes bright—what Maria wouldn't give to have half her friend's glow right about now. She waved, and Fae skipped off, yanking off her apron and shaking out her hair—her petite frame and elfin features catching more than a few lingering stares.

Maria gritted her teeth. She knew this was no environment for her kid, yet it was the only environment they'd known for the last four years. And Mickey was a star. He'd given them a roof over their heads when they'd needed it, jobs too, a life safe from the past. Safe from Fae's father.

And though the men might leer, Fae, just like her mother, knew how to handle them.

Maria just wished her daughter didn't *have* to know.

But then she wished for a lot of things, and wishes were for the foolish, and the hopeful. Not for those who'd been burned enough times in life to think any would come true.

She'd like to think it might be different for Fae though…that one day her daughter might break away and reach for better things. Work to live rather than live to work. Get out of the suburbs and see the world.

'Fae okay?' Trix joined her behind the bar and set about prepping a fresh line of drinks.

'Yeah, she's just tired.'

'Poor darl.' Her phone pinged and she pulled it out of her pocket. 'That girl could do with—' She broke off with a curse.

'What's wrong?'

'I'm still a stew short for next week's charter and my last hope is already at sea.'

'Did you ask Fae?'

'I did but, as you suspected, she turned me down too. Said she'd rather work back-to-back bar shifts than spend a long weekend on water.'

Maria shook her head. It was one thing for her daughter to turn down the lucrative job offer, another to miss out on the added adventure. A change of scene. A new environment that wasn't the same old, day in day out.

'Did she say why?'

'Something about keeping her feet firmly on the ground.'

'I knew she had a fear of flying, but sailing…'

'Anyway, she's out, so are you in?'

'Ha!'

'I'm serious.'

'And so am I.'

'Like daughter, like mother.'

'It's not the sailing I object to.'

'It's just like working here only doing it on water, and you used to be a housekeeper, right? The work will be a breeze in comparison to this place.'

It wasn't the work she was objecting to either.

'It means leaving Fae alone…'

'You were going to trust her with me on a yacht for a few days.'

'That's different. I'd hoped she'd enjoy it. See it as an adventure.'

'She'd probably enjoy having her own space at home more. She's eighteen—an adult. You have to stop mollycoddling her.'

'I don't—'

Trix cocked a brow.

'Okay, I do. Maybe. Just a little. But she's my baby girl.'

'And she'll always be your baby girl, but these

charter guests have deep pockets. You could earn enough to take you and Fae on holiday. Have some real mother and daughter time outside of this place.'

'A holiday?' She huffed out. 'What's one of those again?'

'My point exactly. And how do you expect Fae to go off and live her life if you won't do the same?'

Maria's mouth twisted up.

'And Bob is just across the hall, she can call him if she has any issues, and in the meantime, you can have some fun on board a superyacht with me.'

'Fun?'

'Yeah, Montgomery, the owner, he's pretty chill. I reckon we might even get some beach time in.'

Fun. Sun. A whole heap of money. She'd be a fool to say no. And she knew Trix was right about Fae. How could she expect her daughter to leave these four walls if she herself wouldn't?

'And before you say it, Uncle Mickey can already cover the shifts. I checked before asking Fae.'

'You have an answer for everything.'

Trix grinned. 'It's the only way to be, so you in?'

'Hey, hot stuff, is that drink going to walk itself over, or shall I come round there and get it?'

Maria blinked to find Table Four stood where Fae had once been, his eyes now glassy up close. Not his first bar of the evening then…

She gave Trix a nod. 'Yeah, I'm in.'

Then sliding his drink across the bar, she gave a well-versed smile. 'Can I get you some chips, pretzels, nuts to go with that?'

'You upselling me?'

'You look like you could do with something more substantial than beer.'

He took up his drink. 'Are you offering your services?'

She cocked a brow. 'My services?'

His gaze dipped to her chest.

'I'd quit that thought right now if you know what's good for you.'

'Everything okay here, Maria?' Bob appeared from the back and the guy immediately backed away.

'All good, mate. All good.'

She set her exasperated smile on Bob. 'I had him handled, you know.'

'Yeah, you did,' Trix cheered as Bob grunted.

'Yeah, well, I didn't fancy breaking up a fight this evening.'

Maria laughed as she cleared the empties off the tray Fae had left. 'He would've been asking for it.'

'You say that every time.'

'Well, they shouldn't underestimate a woman.'

'Sometimes I fear you underestimate them too.'

The bar door swung open, and she glanced up—everything in her stilled, then kicked into overdrive at the sight of the man stepping inside. Now *he* was a whole different kind of trouble.

Bob nodded his way. 'Looks like someone took a wrong turn.'

'I'm sure he'll work it out soon enough.'

Because a guy dressed like that didn't belong in a joint like this...

Suave, sophisticated, swanky suit and tie.

Trix's superyacht, yeah. Mickey's bar, no.

'Or not,' she added, her bemused smile spreading as the guy's gaze landed squarely on her. A shallow breath, two...and then he was striding towards her.

'You know him?' Bob asked.

'No.'

And he had a face you couldn't forget.

'He sure acts like he knows you...'

'Or *wants* to get to know you,' Trix murmured.

'He can *want* all he likes...'

Trix laughed. 'Now I just feel sorry for him.'

Bob gave a low rumble—possibly a laugh, maybe a warning. 'I'm almost done out back, you come get me if you need me.'

'Will do,' Maria said, only half aware of him disappearing behind her as she stiffened her spine and refused to acknowledge the little skip to her pulse as her body appreciated all that was coming towards her.

Strong chiselled face. Salt-and-pepper hair. Carefully groomed stubble. And eyes…it was those that held her captive. Piercing as they remained fixed on her, their colour impossible to identify across the distance, but she could feel their interest—blatant and hot with it.

Tiny flutters kicked up in her abdomen and she promptly quashed the lot. He was *definitely* trouble. The kind of trouble that belonged firmly in her past.

She had no time for it in her present.

No desire for it in her future.

Zero. Zilch. Zippo!

If someone had asked him where he was, Tim would have struggled to answer. He hadn't been ready to head to his hotel room. And he hadn't wanted to stay where he'd run the risk of bumping into someone else he knew. So he'd taken a cab out of the city and then he'd walked.

Walked and walked, until eventually he'd come across a dated little side street with an equally dated little rock bar and found himself inside.

Thirsty for a drink with no questions on the side.

Thirsty for a time in his life before he'd made his money, before he'd fallen in love, before his responsibilities had multiplied exponentially and he'd forgotten how to sit still. Be happy. Just be.

Thirsty for...peace.

But the brunette with the caramel highlights and eyes of the same warm colour had him thirsty for something else entirely, the sensation so sudden and so shocking he'd rocked back on his heels. Then she'd smiled and it had streaked right through him, warming parts of his body he'd thought long since dead.

His lips had curved up, his legs had moved and he was at the bar before he knew what he was about.

'You lost?' she said.

'Do I look lost?'

'You really want me to answer that?'

She plucked a glass off the side, expertly polishing it with a cloth as her fiery gaze drifted over him. He couldn't remember the last time he'd been looked at with such...not hostility, but something. And it sure as hell had him *feeling* something in return.

He scanned the rest of the joint—the array of rock shirts on display, the gruff beards and piercings aplenty—and slackened off his tie.

'Oh, yeah, that helps,' she said with a wry twist of her luscious pink lips. 'What can I get you?'

He checked the array of spirits on the mirror-backed wall. 'Johnny Walker Black. Neat.'

'Sure thing, sugar.'

Sugar? He wanted to laugh. He'd never been called sugar in his life.

'You want to take a seat and I'll bring it over?'

'I'd rather sit here, if it's all the same to you.'

She shrugged. 'Suit yourself.'

He slid onto the bar stool, his mouth still tugging at the corners as he watched her grab the bottle off the shelf and slap a glass down in front of him.

'So,' she said as she poured a double without asking, 'what did you do? Bail on your bride-to-be?'

'W—what?' he laughed out.

'The penguin suit, the neat whisky—gotta be on the run.'

Was she serious? Or teasing?

'I think, technically, I need to be wearing a bow tie for this to be classed as a penguin suit.'

Her lips pursed off to the side—was she trapping a laugh? A laugh at *his* expense?

'Whatever.' She slid the glass his way. 'You're a long way from home.'

'Is that a problem?'

'No, everyone's welcome so long as they're not bringing trouble with them.'

'Define trouble.'

'A jilted bride. An angry father, brother, mother…'

'So a lone guy walks into your bar and you immediately leap to wedding?'

'No…' elbows planting onto the bar top, her

eyes sparkled up at him '…a guy walks into my bar in a tux and orders a whisky neat, *then* I leap to wedding.'

'Not a fan?'

'I'm not the one in need of a whisky straight up.'

'Just the one jumping to conclusions.'

'Very true.'

'If you must know—'

'Which I don't…'

'Noted.' The impulsive smile made a return. 'I've come from an event in the city.'

'And chose to finish off your night here?'

'I wouldn't say I chose *per se*…more that I found myself here by chance.'

'So you *are* lost?'

'If one can be lost on purpose, yes.'

He took a sip of his drink, acknowledging that Connor probably had it right ordering the Macallan. Though the pleasing warmth of the drink had nothing on the heat of her gaze as it slid down his throat.

'Mind if I ask why?'

'Thought you said you didn't want to know.'

'I lied.'

'Do you make a habit of lying?'

'Only when it suits me.'

He chuckled. A real, genuine chuckle. The sound as surprising as it was rare. He could almost imagine the look on Sasha's face had she witnessed it. Connor's too.

'Duly noted. Again.'

'So…?'

He sensed the other barmaid leaning closer, the sidelong glances of the other patrons too, and shifted on the stool. Maybe he *should've* taken his drink to a discreet corner. Ducked out of sight, just like he had at his own party.

And here she was asking him why he'd done just that, and he was struggling to come up with an answer that wasn't the plain ugly truth…

But hell, he was tired of denying it.

And what harm was there in admitting it to a stranger anyway? A stranger who he wouldn't see again come tomorrow. A stranger with a smile that had the power to make him feel again. Feel and forget.

However temporary that relief might be…

CHAPTER TWO

GOD, HIS *EYES*...

Maria struggled to look away from the ghosts lurking in their stormy-grey depths.

'Would you think me a coward if I said I was running from my reality?'

'A coward?'

She frowned. No, she'd say he was being brave. Admitting as much to her. Risking his masculinity to show such weakness. Putting a voice to what half this room likely wouldn't, even though they were probably doing the exact same.

Four years ago, she'd done it herself. Run from her life. And she understood why, knew those demons of old. What were his? And could he outrun them like she had?

'Do you want to talk about it?'

The question slipped out before she could stop it, driven by the memory of what it had been like for her, having no one to confide in. How lonely she'd felt, how trapped...

'Does anyone ever want to talk about what pains them?'

'Sometimes.' She shrugged. 'It's what us bar tenders are good for, pouring drinks and lending ears.'

Though lending an ear to him…with the way he made her feel by look alone…she'd be better off letting Trix step in. Before the rebellious little flutters within danced her headlong into trouble.

'Though if you'd rather not…'

She started to move away but he reached out, the gesture turning every flutter into a full-on surge. The warmth consuming her as she blinked up at him.

'Actually…' He wet his lips, the action like pouring gasoline on the already simmering fire within—*Trouble, Maria! Total trouble!* 'At the risk of sounding in need of therapy, that might be kind of healthy.'

She gave an edgy laugh. 'You sure about that, because your face says otherwise?'

'Talking is a new one on me.'

She considered him quietly. 'Yeah, I imagine it is. Consider me honoured.'

'You should be.' He gave a tight chuckle. 'My daughter's been trying to get me to talk to someone for years.'

'Daughter?' Her knees weakened. Her heart too. 'Yeah.'

He took a swig of his whisky, and she checked

his left hand. No ring. Though that didn't mean he wasn't married, or was once, or wasn't still with his daughter's mother. And hell, her head was spinning as much as her heart.

'What about her mum?'

A shadow fell across his face, taking up camp in his ghost-ridden eyes.

'She died.'

His pain reached across the bar, clawing at Maria's chest, stealing her voice.

'Seven years ago.'

Regret slammed into her. 'I'm so sorry.'

He let out a slow breath. 'Yeah, me too.'

'Is she—is she the reason you don't talk?'

'When everyone around you knows about your loss and either tiptoes around it or wants to make it the focus of every conversation, talking loses its appeal.'

'Even now? Seven years on…?'

'Even now, because the talk becomes that of moving on, and I have less interest in moving on than I had talking about it in the first place.'

'Of course…'

'And when it's coming from your own daughter too…'

She pulled a face. 'Ouch. How old is she?'

'Twenty-five. And she likes to think she knows better than her forty-eight-year-old father.'

'Ha. Tell me about it.'

'You too?'

'My daughter's eighteen going on eighty.'

'Dad around?'

'No, thank God.' And she meant that with every fibre of her being. 'We're better off without him in our lives, believe me.'

'Do *you* want to talk about it?'

She gave a tight laugh. 'Hell, no.'

He raised his drink. 'To stories we'd rather not share and daughters who think they know best.'

She gave a soft smile. 'Cheers to that.'

'Can I buy you a drink to toast with?'

'I don't drink on duty.'

'After then?'

She bit her lip. It was tempting. *So* tempting.

And she hadn't been tempted by a man in years.

She didn't *want* to be tempted by a man now.

So what in the hell was she doing indulging in this?

Wake up, Maria!

'I better not, thanks, though.' She pushed back from the bar. 'Enjoy your whisky.'

And then she walked, fighting a backward glance or several.

'Okay, spill!' Trix demanded as she approached.

'Spill what?' Maria said as she kept on walking, putting as much distance between her and him as she sought refuge at the other end of the bar.

'I don't know, his entire life story. You chatted long enough. Looked to be an intense convo from over here.'

She laughed it off. 'Hardly!'

'And now he keeps checking you out.'

'No, he does not.'

Trix raised a brow. 'And you've been back all of ten seconds and looked back just as much.'

Maria flicked a tea towel at her. 'I have not!'

'Have so! And I gotta say if he was looking at me like that,' Trix said out of the corner of her mouth while pulling a beer, 'I wouldn't be in any hurry to leave his side.'

'Trix!'

'What? He's hot.'

'He's also a widower grieving for his wife seven years down the line.'

'Nooo...' She slammed the tap to off and pressed a hand to her chest. 'I think he just got even hotter.'

'I'd tell you that's insensitive, but I fear it would land on deaf ears.'

'And you expect me to believe you're not interested,' she drawled, shoving the schooner in front of the waiting customer and taking payment.

'I'm not!'

'Pull the other one, darl.'

Maria rolled her eyes. 'I'm beginning to regret asking Mickey for extra help tonight.'

'You love having me here really.'

'Debatable.' Though she smiled as she said it, nodding to a fresh customer and taking his order.

'Come on, darl,' Trix said in her ear while she

served. 'Don't tell me you're not itching to un-wrap him.'

'Hell, no.' She shivered, fearing it was more through the thrill of it, than repulsion. 'Men with his kind of money, his kind of charm, they're a recipe for disaster and I want no part of it.'

She'd been there, lost her heart, and almost broke her daughter in the fallout. She'd be a fool to go there again.

'So you discussed his bank balance then?'

'What? No! You can just tell these things…'

'Sounds a little prejudiced to me.'

'I'm not prejudiced.'

'A man-hater, then.'

'I'm not a man-hater either.'

'You're something, darl, and I'm not entirely sure it's doing you any favours. When was the last time you had a bit of fun in that department?'

'It's not that simple. I have Fae to think about.'

'When it comes to sex, the only person who matters is you.'

Maria choked on her own laugh. 'When you're a mother you'll understand.'

'You saying mothers don't need sex too be-cause—'

'Trix!'

'What? It's healthy to want it. Your problem is you keep insisting the two go hand in hand, sex and relationships. Flings are all about the sex, a temporary rush of meaningless fun. And you

ought to keep that in mind because if I were you...'
she checked him out across the bar '... I'd be lock-
ing him down before he scarpers and leaves you
with nothing but regret.'

'I've no room for any more regret, believe me.'

'I wouldn't be so sure about that.'

Maria glanced in his direction, Trix's words
echoing through her as his eyes lifted to hers and
her breath caught, her cheeks warmed, those areas
of her body that he'd reawakened after so many
years begging to be listened to.

But who was to say he wanted her?

Who was to say it wasn't all in her head?

Her body alone?

Then his eyes dipped over her and the fire in
their depths set her soul alight.

He wanted.

And heaven help her, so did she.

Tim didn't believe in love at first sight. Love was
the kind of thing that took time and patience and
understanding. But he believed in a certain kind
of lust—the kind that felt like a lightning bolt
from above. Sudden, fierce, powerful. And as rare
as rain in the desert.

He'd only ever felt it with Ellie and figured it
was a one-time-only deal. The closest thing to
love at first sight he was ever going to get. Until
now.

And he was pretty convinced she felt it too.

She might have run to the other end of the bar but her gaze kept drifting back. Her words might have said she wasn't interested but her eyes…

He wasn't the kind of man to assume desire. Far be it for him to put words in another person's mouth, but as he met her gaze again, he devoured every other outward sign. The way her mouth parted, her cheeks warmed, her chest lifting with a sudden breath—the bolt?

And she wasn't looking away. Not this time.

The beat of the music, the hum of the people, it all fell away. It was just them and this. The heated thread drawing them together.

Her colleague gave her a nudge—a customer was waiting at the bar. It took a second for her to blink, another for her to snap into action and break the connection.

He shook his head and raked his fingers through his hair. What was wrong with him?

He'd blame the drink for his chaotic thoughts, but he'd hardly touched a drop. Not of his whisky or the champagne flowing at the party. Drunk on lust? Him?

He wanted to laugh at the very idea.

But he *was* something…

And as last orders were called and the customers started to leave, anticipation thrummed through his veins. Her looks became longer, more daring, as though she was contemplating, imagining…

The lights were dialled up and the music dialled down.

Her colleague bade her goodnight as a guy emerged from the back. Big enough to be the muscle of the place, but his white get-up and authoritative air singled him out as the chef. He was showing people the door and Tim would be next.

Time to go.

Whatever this was, it wasn't for him.

He downed the last of his drink and stood, lifting his jacket off the back of the stool, but before he could shrug it on, she was there, her hand on his empty glass, her eyes on him.

'Hi...'

Her voice was softer, less sure now the lights were up and her job was done.

'Hi yourself.'

He scanned her face, the way she bit down on her bottom lip, the way her cheeks filled with colour and her pulse flickered in her neck. Nerves?

'Did you change your mind...about the drink?'

'I guess I did.'

His mouth quirked up. 'You guess?'

'Unless you've changed your mind, because that's—'

'No,' he was quick to say. 'I haven't changed my mind.'

'Maria, you good?' the guy in chef whites called out.

'Yeah, I'm good.' She threw him a smile. 'You get yourself up to bed.'

He gave her a nod, his eyes narrowing on Tim.

'We're just…' Her eyes flitted back to Tim too. 'We're gonna get a drink together.'

'No worries.' Though the guy's gaze suggested he was none too sure about that. 'Holler if you need me.'

'Will do. G'night.'

She waited for him to head out through a door in the back before saying, 'Sorry about that. Bob can be a little overprotective.'

'Only a little?'

Her lips curved up, her eyes warming with affection for the guy. 'He likes to look out for us.'

'You and your daughter?'

'Yeah, he lives across the hall from us, upstairs.'

'That's handy. I mean the living upstairs from work, not the bodyguard across the hall…though on second thoughts, that's pretty handy too.'

She laughed. 'I suppose it is. Though not so handy when it means all your eggs are in one basket.'

'Eggs?'

'My livelihood and my living quarters, especially with the developers closing in, but it is what it is,' And dialling up her smile, she gestured to the bar. 'So, what can I get you to drink?'

'Your shift's over, it's my turn to ask you.'

She studied him for a beat.

'Okay. Give me two minutes to finish clearing up and I'll bring the bottle over.'

'Whisky?'

She cocked a brow, the self-assured barmaid making a return. 'Is that a problem?'

'Of course not.'

'Good,' she said with the same wry twist of her lips. 'For a second there I thought you were going to suggest it's too manly a drink for me.'

'I don't think I'd dare.'

She set his empty glass on the tray. 'Glad to hear it.'

'Can I help clear up?'

'You want to help?'

'Why not?' He took the tray from her grasp. 'I'm more than capable of collecting glasses.'

She grinned as she came out from behind the bar. 'Any breakages and you pay.'

'Wouldn't have it any other way.'

'Off you go then.'

He sensed her watching in bemused stillness as he swept around the room, collecting up the glasses.

'You just going to stand there and watch?'

'I was considering it,' she said, laughing as she moved to lock up the front and pull down the blinds.

She set the lights back to their muted glow and he joined her behind the bar, balancing the heavy tray while handing her the empties to load into the dishwasher. They moved in perfect synch—until his fingers brushed hers. She jolted. He jolted. Their eyes met and the glass fell, shattering against the floor and drowning out their shared curse.

'I'll pay for it,' he said, sliding the tray onto the side and crouching to gather the shards.

'Don't, you'll—'

Too late. He hissed as a sharp fragment pierced his finger.

'Oh, my God!' She dropped to her haunches and reached for his hand. Her sultry, spicy scent washing over him as her fingers wrapped around his wrist…talk about an assault on the senses.

He cleared his throat. 'It's fine.'

'It's not fine,' she blurted, 'you're bleeding.'

'I'll survive.'

'Come with me.' Her tone brooked no argument, and he was in no position to give one, not with her touch licking a fire right through him. They rose as one and she urged him to the sink, turned on the tap to let the water run over it. 'Didn't your mother ever teach you not to mess with broken glass?'

'I wasn't messing, I was helping.'

'Funny kind of helping, making a greater mess for me to tend to.'

She pulled out a first aid kit from under the

counter, his hand still clutched in hers and taking him with her every step of the way.

'Are you calling me a mess?'

Her mouth twitched up as she tended to the cut, checking it for stray glass before pressing a strip of gauze to the fresh well of blood. 'If the shoe fits...'

Their eyes met, her words playful but everything else—her gaze, her care, her touch—this close, this sincere, this *intense*...

'What would you say if this mess told you he wanted to kiss you?'

She drew in a breath, her chest lightly grazing his.

'I'd say nothing.'

'In that case, what would you do?'

She rose on tiptoes, her lashes lowering as her lips inched closer...

'This.'

Boom!

Fireworks. That was what Maria felt as she threw caution to the wind and kissed him. The explosive rush of being this close to another person again, of letting the heat and the need take over. It was everything she'd been missing and everything she'd walk away from again come tomorrow, but right now... Trix was right.

He wrapped his arm around her, tugging her

close, the groan caged within his throat rumbling through her chest.

'You taste like heaven.'

She wanted to laugh, wanted to tell him that was the expensive whisky they'd planned to consume, but they hadn't got to that yet. He had though, and he tasted divine. Lush and masculine. And she couldn't get enough.

'This is crazy,' she said, barely breaking away for fear it would stop.

'If crazy means good, I agree.'

'But your hand…'

'All better, thanks to you.'

His grey eyes seared her, the flush to his handsome cheeks too.

And then she kissed him, deeper, harder, revelling in the heat of his body pressed against hers as she released his hand to bury her own in his hair.

'You should know,' he rasped against her lips as he lifted her onto the counter. 'I don't do this.'

'This?'

'Lose all good sense in a heartbeat.'

She laughed against his mouth, wrapping her legs around him. 'Neither do I.'

'Then what are we doing?'

'I don't know that either.' She leaned back just enough to meet his gaze, the fire in his leaving her as breathless as his kiss. 'I just know I haven't felt like this in a long time, and I don't want you to walk out of here and regret what could have been.'

His eyes dipped to her mouth and back again. 'Ditto.'

'Then maybe we should quit talking,' she said, reaching closer.

'I won't argue.' He supped on her bottom lip, the briefest of caresses that had her thighs flexing around him, her fingers tightening in his hair. 'But if you want me to stop, you only have to—'

'If I want you to stop…' she stared into his eyes as their foreheads locked together, their breaths coming in shallow, synchronised puffs '…you'll know about it. But right now, I'm telling you I want this.'

She sealed her words with a kiss, her hands falling to the buttons of his shirt, fingers trembling as she hurried to undo each one. Safe in the knowledge that this was temporary, and it was mutual.

And for a night she could roll with it. Trust him with it.

She shoved the shirt from his shoulders, her palms recognising before her eyes could see that he was a mortal god. Every muscle honed to perfection. *Holy moly.* She bit into her lip and drank him in.

'Do you think we should…?'

Her eyes shot to his. He gestured to the door.

'It's okay, no one's coming back in here.'

'In that case…' He slid his hands beneath her T, his palms hot and sure as they moved over her skin to the curve of her breasts… Heat rushed to greet his touch, her nipples pressing against the lace of her bra as his thumbs teased each peak.

'You feel so good,' he murmured.

'That *feels* so good.' She arched back, her hands planting into the bar top as her head rolled back. How had she gone so long without this pleasure in her life?

'Do you have protection?'

His question snapped her back to earth. 'No.'

He swore under his breath and her panicked brain raced for a solution. 'The vending machine!'

'The what now?'

She shot off the counter. 'We have a vending machine.'

'You do?'

'In the ladies…'

She pulled him to the till, grabbed some coins. 'Add it to my bill.'

She laughed. 'Oh, I will, don't you worry.'

Then she tugged him into the loos, his chuckle deep and throaty right behind her. 'This is a first for me.'

'The ladies or the vending machine?' she said, slotting in the coins and pressing the button, her hips rolling against him as he closed in.

'Both.'

He wrapped his arms around her, his lips grazing her throat, the rough scrape of his stubble sending tiny ripples of excitement down her spine.

The pack dropped and she snatched it up, turning in his hold as he guided her back against a stall.

'One night, yeah?' she blurted before his lips could claim hers, needing that reassurance, that reminder that this was all it was. A moment of madness, nothing that could hurt and everything they could enjoy as two consenting adults.

No promises. No commitment. Just fun.

He nodded. 'One night.'

CHAPTER THREE

Tɪᴍ ᴡᴀꜱɴ'ᴛ ꜱᴜʀᴇ what roused him from his sleep—the soft snoring in his ear or the warm, silken body wrapped around him. All he knew was that he hadn't known a peace like it in too long. And he didn't want to leave.

Which was a sure sign that he should. Giving into lust was one thing, getting attached again... never.

She stirred, her head travelling down his chest until her cheek rested against his pec, her limbs tightening around him. He exhaled, abandoning all thought of leaving. A few hours wouldn't hurt. The amber glow slipping through her blinds said it was still early. Maybe they could grab coffee, some breakfast. It was Saturday after all—a day of rest for many. Maybe it was time he fell into that habit too.

His phone buzzed beside him and he reached out to silence it.

Okay, so maybe his world didn't agree.

He checked the caller ID. Sasha?

He frowned. She was supposed to be hosting a gala for her charity in London right now. A function that he should be attending too. But his corporate commitments had taken precedence—or at least that was what he'd said.

In reality, he still struggled to walk the same halls Ellie once had and the UK was full of them. Not to mention that the charity itself had been set up in her honour. If ever there was an event where people would want to talk about her, it was there.

A message buzzed through and Maria nuzzled in deeper, setting off a string of vibrations within him. How could he want her again already?

He felt like a hormonal teenager, not a man of his years. *Three* times they'd succumbed. Three times they'd completely lost their minds to it. The last session a very sleepy but very satisfying coming together that had seen her drifting off in his arms and he hadn't wanted to leave. Much like he didn't want to leave now. But he had to check on Sasha.

Easing out from under her, he scanned the room for his clothing. Where on earth…? They'd been otherwise engaged when they'd stumbled in during the night, but it had to be here somewhere. Not that he could see in every corner and he wasn't about to turn on a light.

Giving up, he grabbed the only obvious thing he could find—her kimono off the back of the door—and tugged it on. It would have to do.

Out he crept, straight into the living area where the early morning rays seeped through the thin curtains, bathing everything in gold. For the first time, he truly took in the space… The hodge-podge of old chairs, tables and cabinets that shared no cohesive quality but somehow worked together. Fresh flowers bloomed on the tiny coffee table. Books and plants lined the shelves. Photos too. Most depicting landscapes from around the world, while others were pictures of her and a young girl. Her daughter?

His phone buzzed again, reminding him of his own kid.

Call me back x

He dialled her number and crossed the room to the window, lifting back the curtain to eye the street below. A far cry from the fancy city block he'd left behind, the rundown strip was in dire need of a cash injection. Boarded-up businesses. Overflowing rubbish bins. Graffiti-laden walls. Connor would have a fit if he could see him now…and the thought only made him smile further.

'Dad!'

'Hello to you too, darling,' he murmured, careful to keep his voice down. 'Do you know what time it is?'

'Don't pretend you're not already awake and checking your email.'

'Actually, I—'

'And don't you darling me. Connor says you bailed on your party. The party you told me you couldn't possibly miss to come to the gala.'

He caught sight of his guilt-ridden grimace in the glass. 'Says the girl who's supposed to be at that very same gala now, entertaining her guests, but instead is berating her father for not being there.'

'I got sick of covering for you.'

'Covering for me?'

'Yes. *Everyone* is asking where you are. One day they'll realise that it's me running this charity and not you. Until then, it would be nice not to spend most of my time fielding questions about you.'

'I'm sorry, darling.'

'So am I. Not because of that, but because you're not here. And you should be.'

'Maybe next year.'

'You said that last year and the year before and...'

'I know, I know.'

She fell silent. In the background he could hear the gentle hum of chatter, laughter, music too.

'You should go back to your party.'

'It's really not the same without you here. It helped me, you know, coming back here, seeing the people who helped Mum, being around the family. You can't blame them all for asking where you are, Dad. Gran hasn't seen you since you flew her out to Paris.'

'That was a good trip, we should do it again.'

'It would be a lot easier on her if you came here.'

Sasha was right. Ellie's mum was getting on in years. But visiting her in the home where Ellie grew up, with her pictures in every room and, no, just no.

'Please, Dad.'

He cleared his throat. 'I'll see what I can sort.'

'And while you're doing that, will you sort your diary so that you can get out on the boat with Connor next week? He told me he asked and you flat-out refused.'

'I didn't refuse, I said I'd think about it.'

'Which is code for no.'

'It isn't code, it's an "I'll think about it".'

'You need to get a life, Dad. One that doesn't revolve around work and me.'

'I'm on it.'

Sasha's laugh of disbelief rippled down the phone. 'Being on it would be you saying yes to Connor for a start. He says you've not had a boys' trip in years.'

'Maybe because we're not boys any more—young, free and single.'

'Knock it off, Dad, you're hardly over the hill. And you're definitely free and single.'

'Doesn't make me ready to mingle like he wants to.'

'I know Connor can be a bit wild, but you could do with a little bit of that in your life...'

Hell, if Sasha only knew where he was now. What he *looked* like right now. He tugged at the floral fabric of Maria's kimono. His confession stuck on his tongue.

'Don't you think it's time?' she said softly.

He looked back to the view, though he wasn't seeing the street now. He was seeing the past. A premature goodbye and the guilt at feeling something for another, no matter how different it was.

'Pardon me if I don't want to take life advice from my twenty-five-year-old daughter who should be living her own life rather than interfering in mine.'

'I'm not interfering, I'm advising. There's a difference.'

'Well, whatever you're doing, you need to stop and get back to your party before you're missed. I hear you're set to smash last year's target, you should be proud.'

'I don't do it for me.'

'I'm proud of you, and I can be proud enough for the three of us.'

Because he knew Ellie would have been bursting with pride for all their daughter had achieved.

Hitting the ground running with her charity venture at the young age of twenty and turning it into the multi-million-pound charity it was now, five years on.

'Thanks, Dad.'

He smiled. 'You're welcome, darling. So…how is the party?'

Maria shot up with a start, eyes wide, hands clutching the bedsheets…

Someone had screamed. She was sure of it. But her room was empty, the flat now quiet. Had she imagined it, or had—

'Who the hell are you?'

Her gaze shot to the door—*Fae!*

Oh, God, Tim!

She threw off the covers and darted for the door, pausing belatedly to snatch her kimono off the back and grasping thin air. She stared at the empty hook. What the—

'Mum!'

'I can explain,' came Tim's voice.

'I very much doubt that! Mum! What are you wearing? Is that—is that *Mum's*?'

Oh, God, oh, God, oh, God. She dashed around the bedroom, pulling on her knickers and grabbing the first thing that came to hand—his shirt, half-visible beneath the bed! Shoving her arms in, she buttoned it as she raced out.

Fae was in her bedroom doorway. Tim was before the living room window. Her floral kimono, a ridiculous sight on his too tall, too broad frame. What was he *thinking*, wearing *that*?

'Mum?'

'It's okay, Fae.'

She raised a placating hand while running the other through her hair that felt as wild as her daughter's looked.

'Is *it*?' Fae wrapped her arms around her py-jama-clad middle, eyes brimming with accusation as she pinned Tim with a glare. 'Who the hell is this?'

'This…' She glanced his way, wishing she'd woken sooner, wishing she'd thought to exercise more caution, wishing for anything but the current situation.

She wasn't about to wish the night away though… she wasn't an idiot and Fae wasn't a child. She was still her kid though and this was her home too. She had a right to be upset at his presence.

'This is Tim,' she said, like that explained everything, copying Fae's crossed arm stance and wishing his shirt was thicker, longer…that her kimono wasn't showing off far too much of him.

Hell, she needed to explain properly, but she couldn't think straight. Not when her body was overheating with remembered scenes from the night before, of the things he'd done, that *she'd* done—

'Since we're all up, shall I put the coffee on?'

She averted her gaze and made a run for the machine. Coffee made everything better.

'Coffee?' Fae squeaked.

'Do you have tea?' Tim said.

'Do we have *tea*?' Fae repeated, mimicking his accent that had suddenly become very English. Maria was sure he'd sounded Aussie the night before. Maybe he was an ex-pat, or so well-travelled he'd picked up various accents along the way. It only served to highlight how little she knew about him and how reckless she had been, and now she was seeing it all through Fae's eyes maybe regret *should* be more forthcoming.

'I'm afraid not,' Maria said, loading the coffee machine and sensing her daughter's aghast frown continuing to flit between them.

'Did you— Did he— Did...'

Maria's head snapped in her direction—*for the love of God, don't say it!*

Fae shook her head, her cheeks colouring. 'I don't believe this.'

Then she turned and fled to her room, the slam of her door making them both flinch.

'Oh, God,' Maria grumbled. 'Shoot me now.'

'I'm so sorry,' he said.

'You have nothing to be sorry for...'

Maria, on the other hand. So much for no regrets.

'Oh, I do.' He came towards her and her pulse kicked up. How could she still find him hot in *that*? 'I think I'd be the same if I came across me dressed like this.'

He gave her a smile that had her toes curling into the wooden floor, warmth swirling through her lower belly despite her unease. Seriously! How was it possible? Anyone else and she'd be laughing at the ridiculous sight he made...

'It shouldn't look good on you, but...'

She reached out, her hand coming to rest upon his chest as her eyes lifted to his. Her intention had been to stop whatever he'd been about to do. Instead, the feel of his hot, hard body through the silk had her wishing for it all.

'I know what you mean,' he said, lifting his fingers to the open collar of the shirt she wore, the lightest sweep of his fingers against her collarbone making her breath quiver. 'My shirt will never look plain again.'

She wet her lips—*take it down a notch, take—it—down!*

'Mind telling me *why* you chose my kimono?'

'It was the quickest thing to hand.'

'In a rush to escape me?'

'My daughter called.' He raised his phone. 'I didn't want to risk waking you.'

'Oh...' Thoughtful, sweet, the reminder that he was a parent too—a *caring* one—warming her in other ways.

'I have a feeling she'll be calling back very

soon demanding an explanation for the girl she could hear screaming in the background.'

She grimaced. 'She heard?'

'Oh, yes, she heard.'

'What did you tell her?'

'That I was with a friend.'

'A *screaming* friend?'

'Hence why I'll have questions of my own to answer soon enough.'

'I'm sorry.' Maria glanced at Fae's door. 'She isn't used to me bringing men home.'

'You said as much last night, though it's nice to know I truly am a special case.'

A special case that you were supposed to be waving bye-bye to come morning...

She pulled away, freeing herself of his touch as much as his gaze.

'Dressed in that, definitely,' she said, deploying humour as a shield.

He gave a gruff laugh. 'Okay, there's only so much teasing a man's ego can take. Do you mind if I shower?'

'Help yourself.' The sooner she had space, the better. 'Towels are in the cupboard behind the door, use whatever you need.'

'Cheers.'

She set the coffee going and leaned back against the counter, taking a breath, then another, seeking calm and finding the opposite.

One night wasn't supposed to become a morning too. A morning where she craved it turning into another and another...

'Is he taking a *shower* now?'

Her head snapped up to find Fae gawping at her from across the room, hazel eyes firing sparks.

'Yes.'

Fae cursed.

'Language!'

'I need the loo!'

'He won't be long.'

'He's been here too long already.'

'I invited him.' Maria sighed. 'If you want to be mad at anyone, be mad at me.'

'I *am* mad at you!'

Maria's mouth fell open. She scrambled for something to say, something that wouldn't make the situation worse. Because truth was, she'd enjoyed having him with her for the night, and the whole point had been to indulge in a little fun and wake up with no regrets.

Not have them pile on by the plenty.

'I'm sorry, Mum,' Fae suddenly blurted, her shoulders slumping, eyes softening as she stepped forward. 'I don't mean to be...to be an arse. But I got up to get a glass of water, I walk in here and get the fright of my life. You could've at least warned me you had someone coming back.'

'I know, I'm sorry. It wasn't like I planned it. He came into the bar for a drink last night and we got talking and things...things just happened.' She bit her lips together as her daughter's eyes fired once more. 'What I mean is—'

'What you mean is, you just hooked up with some *random* guy? A guy you didn't even *know* before last night?'

Maria felt her cheeks burn. Who was the mother in this relationship?

'I know it looks bad but…'

'Too right it looks bad, you'd blow a fuse if I'd done that.'

'That's different.'

'How? *How* is that different?'

Her daughter had a point. 'I'm your mother for a start.'

'You are and you should know better.'

No argument there…

'Who even is he? He sounds like a right stuck-up—'

'*Fae*,' she warned.

'What, Mum? We know his type. He'll use you to get what he wants and leave you for dust when he's done.'

'Keep your voice down, love, he'll hear you.'

'I don't care if he hears me. He's gonna be just like all the rest. Just like…'

'He's *not* your father.'

'Yeah, well, don't say I didn't warn you.'

'You don't need to warn me, I know well enough.'

'Bullsh—'

'Fae! It was just a night, honey, nothing more.'

And now she was stressing she'd indulged in a one-night stand. To her own *daughter*. For crying out loud, could this get any worse?

Fae frowned. 'You're *not* planning on seeing him again?'

She shook her head, the 'no' sticking in her throat.

'Okay.' Fae raised her chin, gave a nod. 'Good.'

It was good. So why did it feel like anything but…?

'It's not that I don't want you to be happy, Mum. But this is our life. We spent so long living under Dad's thumb and now we're finally free of him and have things just how we want them… To have another man come in and…'

She broke off, her bottom lip quivering, and Maria was across the room in a heartbeat.

'Oh, honey, come here…' She pulled Fae into her arms. 'I am never letting a man take control of our lives again. I promise you that.' She kissed her hair. 'This is our home. Yours and mine. Okay?'

Fae sniffed against her chest, nodded. 'Yeah.'

She held her for a long moment, centring her thoughts on Fae and their life and why there was no room for a man. Especially one as distracting and all-consuming as Tim.

'You know he was talking to another "*dah-ling*" on the phone when I came in…' Fae murmured, glancing up at her. 'A bit dodge, don't you think?'

She gave a twisted smile. 'His daughter. Not another woman.'

'How can you know that for sure?'

She couldn't, not really. Just because he'd *told* her he didn't do this often didn't make it true. People made great liars when it suited them. Fae's father, Fraser, had been one of the best. He'd fooled her. And he'd fooled his wife. For years they'd danced to the tune of his lies and she wouldn't dance to the tune of another now, lies or otherwise.

The door to the bathroom swung open and he emerged in a cloud of steam, the look on his face telling her he'd overheard plenty. Bugger.

'I'll just throw my clothes on and get out of your hair.'

She nodded, unable to trust her voice. Especially when faced with him in nothing more than a towel, his hair and skin still wet, grey eyes shimmering with an emotion she didn't want to explore but felt to her core...

Damn it. He made her feel, made her want, made her put another first in the heat of the night—and that was why he had to go.

End of.

CHAPTER FOUR

TIM KNEW ENOUGH of teenage girls to know that Fae wasn't acting out because of him. He was pretty sure any man would have elicited the same response.

Even so, he dressed as quickly as he could. Stalling when he realised Maria still wore his shirt. As much as some men might consider a dinner jacket and trousers an outfit, he wasn't one.

But thinking of her in it...the way the white fabric fell to mid-thigh, shifting against her skin as she moved...he cursed as his body tightened.

So many years of zero interest in women and now he couldn't put a lid on it. What was that saying about Pandora's Box? And why the hell did that feel a euphemism? He groaned as he dragged a hand down his face, slapped his cheeks.

Get a grip!

He just needed to get his shirt and get the hell out of there. He glanced at the door, more than aware of the women still talking on the other side. He'd hoped Fae might disappear again, hide out until he was gone. More for the girl's benefit than his. But it wasn't to be...

Pocketing his phone, he grabbed his jacket off the floor and headed out. He found them in the kitchen, sipping coffee, the mood in the air suffocatingly thick as they both turned to him.

He cleared his throat, feeling every exposed millimetre of his chest. 'I'm going to need that back...'

He gestured to her—*his* shirt.

'Oh, God, of course! Sorry!' She slapped her mug down. 'I'll just change.'

She hurried from the room and the temperature dropped to freezing. Why the hell hadn't he thought to follow her?

Fae muttered something under her breath, her hostile glare enough to make him want to wilt— *Wilt*, him?

Be a man, for Pete's sake. Own it. Apologise. Move on.

He couldn't be afraid of an eighteen-year-old... could he?

'I really am sorry,' he tried.

'Yeah, you and me both.'

Okay, maybe he was, a little...

He rocked on his feet, paying great attention to the furnishings—the scuffed leg of the coffee table, the stitched-up sofa cushion, the damp seeping into the corner wall... Maria hurried back in, thank God!

Now dressed in shorts and an oversized T that had seen better days, she was a sight for sore eyes.

'There you go,' she said, passing him his shirt and snapping around as Fae tried to sneak out behind her. 'Where are you going?'

'I'm going to take my coffee to the park. That okay?'

'You don't have to go,' he said, tossing his jacket on the sofa and pulling on his shirt. 'I'll call a cab and be gone in—'

'It's fine,' she said to her mum. 'I want to get some air, and it'll give you chance to see *him*... off!'

She made it sound like he was about to *be* offed, particularly as she grunted the word while tugging on the door that was in dire need of a good planing.

He swallowed a crazed laugh and buttoned up his shirt. All the assurances he wanted to give about not being *that* guy—the guy to take the sex and run—dying on his lips because, a, that was precisely what they had agreed to do. And b, she looked in no mood to hear it.

The door slammed shut and Maria pressed a hand to her mouth, the other fisted on her hip as she stared after her daughter. Was she upset? Nervous? Mortified? All of the above?

Whatever the case, she was no longer the confident barmaid willing to give in to the chemistry that had taken them both by surprise last night...

No, she was Maria the mum and the father in him could understand that and sure as hell sympathise.

'Funny how our kids can bring us back to earth with such gravitas.'

'Gravitas?' She gave a tight laugh as she turned to him. 'That's one word for it.'

'Anyone else dare judge us for last night,' he said, tucking in his shirt, 'and we'd tell them where to go, but our kids…'

Her smile twisted off to the side as she gave a slow nod. 'Yeah…'

'You're okay though?' he asked, the idea that she was now regretting what had been one of the best nights of his life giving him pause.

'I will be.' She glanced up at him, her smile not half as bright or as easy as he wanted it to be. 'Can I get you a coffee?'

'It's okay.' He was more than aware he'd overstayed his welcome. 'I can get one on the road.' He took up his phone, opened the app to request a taxi. 'It shouldn't take long to get a cab.'

'Honestly, it's no bother. At least have a coffee while you wait.'

He glanced up. 'Are you sure?'

She nodded. 'Fae won't come back until she knows you're gone if that's what you're worried about…'

He searched her gaze. 'I'm more concerned

about what you want and whether you're only offering to be nice.'

She gave a laugh, her eyes sparkling with it. Now *that* was the woman he'd met last night. 'You should know, I don't do anything for nice's sake.'

'Well, in that case...' he returned her smile '... I'd love one.'

She headed to the kitchenette while he chose a cab twenty minutes away. Long enough not to drink and run, short enough not to become any more of a burden. He pocketed his phone and browsed the photos on her shelves while he waited.

Most were of cities around the world, interspersed with photos of Fae, or her and Fae together. He picked one off the shelf, smiling at the heartwarming moment captured between mother and daughter.

'That was the day we moved in here,' she said as she handed him a mug. 'Mickey took it.'

'Mickey?'

'The owner of the building, he owns the bar too.'

'Nice guy?'

'One of the best.'

His brows twitched as he kept his focus on the pic and his thoughts to himself. Because in his honest opinion, Mickey needed a lesson in How to be a Responsible Landlord if the damp and the dodgy door were anything to go by. The memory of them crashing through it the night before flashed through his mind and he promptly quashed it.

'If it wasn't for him—well, let's just say back then, we needed him more than he needed us.'

Why? He wanted to ask. But questions like that…they were hardly easy morning chat, easy goodbye chat. And that was what they were supposed to be doing.

He placed the photo back down. 'It's a great picture.'

'It was a great day.'

Her eyes warmed, her smile reminiscent.

'How so?' he couldn't stop himself from asking and immediately tried to backtrack, 'Or does this come under the same banner as the ex you'd prefer to forget?'

'It *is* the same banner as the ex.'

She sipped her coffee and he figured she was done, but then she surprised him with more. 'Up until then, he wasn't just in our life, he controlled it. Where we lived. Who we saw. Where Fae went to school. It took a lot to break away. But once we had…' She sighed. 'I'm afraid it's part of the reason she was so hard on you.'

Her explanation should have made him feel better. The confirmation that it wasn't about *who* he was, rather than *what* he was. A threat.

'I'm only sad that I didn't see sense sooner. I could have saved her a lot of heartache.'

'I don't know,' he said softly. 'It's hard when you live with someone for so long to imagine life without them. Whether the relationship is good or bad, it's what you know.'

'We never lived together, not in the way you're thinking…' She licked her lips, shifting tempo as she walked away. 'And this is way too deep a conversation to be having over our morning coffee.'

'I'd like to have it though,' he said, following her. 'If you're willing to talk about it.'

So much for keeping it light and easy…

But damn it, he *wanted* to know. Maybe it was because she'd got him talking about Ellie. Maybe it was because she got him feeling like Ellie once had. Maybe it was because he wasn't ready to walk away, no matter that his survival instincts said to do otherwise.

'You know we're not friends, right. You don't have to be all sweet and interested just because we…' she nudged her head towards the bedroom and he urged his mind not to travel in the same direction '…hooked up.'

'Hooked up?' He gave a chuckle as tight as his body now felt. 'It's been a long time since I hooked up with anyone.'

'Really? Because last night you seemed to know your way around like an expert.'

Her cheeks glowed, her eyes too, and hell, it took every bit of restraint not to tug her to him and work his way around her all over again.

'I could say the same about you.'

She laughed with him. 'Some skills you never unlearn, I guess.'

'I think it's more about the person than the skills. A rare connection that just...works.' He held her gaze as he accepted the truth. He didn't just want to talk today, he wanted to see her again tomorrow and quite possibly the next and the next. 'Maria, I know we said this was a—'

'Don't say it,' she blurted.

'You don't know what I'm going to say yet.'

'It's written in your face.'

'It is?'

'*Yes.* And I can't.'

'Why?'

'I just can't. We agreed. One night and then you go your way, I go mine. No complications. No muddying the waters and making this into more than it needs to be.'

'That still doesn't answer my question—why can't we see each other again?'

'I... I don't want to.'

Maria stared up into his grey eyes while her head screamed, *'Liar!'*

Yes, she wanted to see him again. Yes, she wanted to continue this conversation. Out here, back in the bedroom, wherever and whenever he wanted it to happen. And that was all the warning she needed.

'I don't want to see you again,' she repeated, as much for her own benefit as his, 'because there's no room in my life for a man.'

'You make it sound like I'm after forever.'

She choked on a laugh. *Imagine?*

'Not forever, no...' Though his words weren't too dissimilar to Trix's, berating her for seeing sex and relationships as one and the same thing. 'But I think it would be unfair of me to say yes, when I barely have a moment spare for me and Fae as it is. My life revolves around her and working to keep a roof over our heads.'

'Everyone needs some downtime.'

'Are you talking about work or parenthood now, because any decent parent knows you never get off that particular rollercoaster of responsibility?'

'No, our worlds revolve around them, for sure. And when they're young, when they need us, they come first absolutely. But she's eighteen now, she has her own life to lead, and so do you.'

Wasn't that another flavour of what Trix had been saying to her? Though Trix had been more about leading by example and showing her daughter there's more to life than this place and work.

'I know that, believe me, I do.'

But getting caught up in whatever this was between her and Tim, that wasn't the example she wanted to set. In fact, it was the exact opposite. She wanted to show Fae she could do it all on her own. Having spent over a decade with her happiness hinging on Fraser, she wanted Fae to know that she didn't need a man to be happy. That she didn't need a man to secure her future, to have fun either.

'But this is hardly setting her the best example.'

He gave an abrupt laugh. 'No, I don't think this morning was our finest parental hour either, but given time to adjust, time to...'

His voice trailed off as she shook her head. 'I can't.'

She knew from experience just how vulnerable you were at eighteen and she wanted to be there for her daughter, not distracted by him. She was already starting to hate herself enough for exposing Fae to Tim's kimono-clad self that morning...

And that wasn't his fault, it was hers. She'd been the one to bring him back. To put her needs over her daughter in the heat of the moment.

'I'm sorry.'

'No.' He sighed. 'I'm sorry. We agreed this was a one-night deal and I shouldn't be trying to change that up at the eleventh hour.'

He returned to the wall of photos and she watched him go, her heart racing, body and mind adjusting to his acquiescence.

Damn, he was sweet, kind, thoughtful. So freaking understanding and everything Fraser hadn't been.

Which made him even more dangerous....

'You're well-travelled,' he said as she came up alongside him.

'In my dreams.'

He glanced her way. 'You didn't take these?'

'No. It's more a visual bucket list.'

'So, what, you take them off the wall after you've been?'

She sipped her coffee. 'Maybe—I'd have to visit one first.'

'You haven't…'

'I've never been out of Australia. What about you?' she said, swiftly moving on. 'Which ones have you been to?'

He scanned every snap and she got the distinct impression the list was too long to share…or rub in her face.

'Okay.' She gave him a small smile. 'How about telling me your favourite instead?'

He looked back at the wall. 'Impossible to say, they all have different qualities. The gothic beauty of Edinburgh, the romance of Paris, the garden city of Singapore… Have you always wanted to travel?'

'Yeah. As a child, I'd cut pictures out of my mother's magazines, stick them in a scrapbook and tell myself one day I'd get there. I'd escape and see the world.'

'Escape? Is that how you saw it as a kid?'

His eyes narrowed on her and she knew he'd read so much in that one sentence.

She tried to give an easy shrug, but it was awkward, stilted by the memories that never really stayed silent.

'Who doesn't want to escape their home life at times, right?'

'I don't know. If anything, my parents sheltered me, made me feel safe and secure. I was adrift when I first went to boarding school and would fantasise about running back home.'

Her chest warmed with his honesty. 'That's kind of sweet.'

'Not the image you want when you're at boarding school, believe me. It forced me to grow up and find my feet though. What about you?'

'Well, I didn't go to boarding school,' she joked, then admitted softly, 'But I think I would've liked it.'

'Because it wasn't home?'

She gave a soft huff. 'Yeah.'

'Why?'

'That's a tale for another day…'

The day that wasn't ever going to happen. She knew it. He knew it. Time to move on. Because she wasn't dredging up that sorry tale to have him pity her more.

'Where are you from?' she asked. 'Originally, I mean. You sounded English just now, when you said "tea"…' She couldn't help mimicking him like Fae had done. 'But I would have pegged you as a fellow Aussie last night.'

'I'm from Sydney,' he said, taking her change of topic and running with it, though she sensed his question still hanging in the air between them. 'I lived in England for a while. My wife, Ellie, she was English. We met while I was there on business, fell in love, and the rest, as they say...'

'Is history,' she finished softly.

He nodded. 'Sasha, my daughter, she went to school there too.'

'Where's home for you both now?'

'Sasha splits her time between the UK and Sydney.'

'And you?'

'I travel a lot with work. I don't really consider myself as having a base any more.'

'Hence the yo-yo accent.'

'Yo-yo?'

'Yeah, from Aussie to English and whatever else you have going on there.'

'I guess *tea* is one of those words that's quintessentially British.'

She cocked a brow. 'Quintessentially?'

'You know, if I'd known my dialect was going to take this kind of beating come morning, I would have left in the night,' he teased, the weighted mood lifting with it and then shifting into something else as he sobered. 'Do you wish I had?'

The one question she couldn't answer. Not truthfully at any rate. Because it would be so easy to slip into the other truth, that she didn't want him to leave. That she wanted to let this chemistry run its course and pay no heed to what came next. A risk she refused to take.

His phone buzzed and she looked to where it sat in his pocket. 'Do you think that's your ride?'

He stared back at her. 'I guess I have my answer then.'

'It's not that I didn't enjoy last night, Tim.'

'I know, I believe you.'

'I hope so.'

She gave him a weak smile and he threw back the rest of his coffee, grabbed his jacket off the sofa and placed his mug next to the sink. She was waiting for him at the door, tugging the stubborn thing open.

'You really should get that seen to.'

'Tell me something I don't already know.'

'That you are quite wonderful, Maria. And whatever last night was for you, it meant something to me. So, thank you.'

He leant in to sweep a soft kiss against her cheek and she inhaled her own shampoo on his hair, felt his warmth caress her, and then he was gone. And *oh,* how she wanted to run after him. Tell him she'd changed her mind.

But the last time she'd succumbed to a connection like this, a connection that felt like it was meant to be, she'd stumbled away broken. Her daughter suffering all the more for being the unwanted product of an affair. Fraser choosing his *real* family over Fae, protecting them, putting them first.

And Maria had sworn Fae would never feel second-best again. Her daughter was everything. And that was how it would stay.

'Goodbye, Tim,' she whispered into the hallway that was as empty as her chest now felt.

'He's gone then?'

Her head snapped around to find Fae stepping out of Bob's across the way.

'I thought you said you were going to the park.'

'Yeah, I lied.'

Maria shook her head. 'Get back in here.'

Suitably sheepish, Fae crossed the hall and wrapped her arms around Maria's waist.

She hugged her daughter tight. 'Are we good?'

'We're always good, Mum. I love you.'

She kissed her hair. 'I love you too.'

And that was all that mattered. Her and Fae. Tim was just a distraction, a tiny blip. She'd forget about him soon enough…honestly, she would.

'Fancy pancakes with all the trimmings for breakfast?'

Fae's head shot up. 'Now you're talking!'

CHAPTER FIVE

'SO SORRY I'M LATE, TRIX.' Maria barrelled on board the yacht, tugging her small suitcase with her. 'Some surveyor rocked up at the flat as I was trying to leave and I had to show him in.'

'A surveyor? Uncle Mickey finally putting some money back into the place?'

'It would seem that way.'

'Huh.' She nodded. 'Things must be looking up.'

'Let's hope so, yeah.' She paused on deck and looked around, a low whistle escaping. The sleek black vessel was by far the most exclusive-looking yacht currently docked. Bold and daring and radiating wealth... 'How rich did you say this guy was again?'

'I don't know, world's rich list rich. I'd give you a full tour but the boss is due on board any minute and you need to change. I'll point out the main areas on the way to our cabin and the rest we'll pick up later.'

'Sounds good, I'm sure I'll get my bearings soon enough.'

She followed Trix inside, working hard to stop her mouth from hanging open as she listened to her point out various things.

Get my bearings soon—yeah, right! This thing was huge! Huge *and* luxurious. Split over several floors, too.

From the apparent helipad and swimming pool up top, to the state-of-the-art gym, spa pool—yes, two pools!—cinema room, dancefloor, multiple bars and dining areas, before one even got to the master staterooms and VIP suites. This superyacht had everything anyone could want. And with its teak floors, sumptuous furnishings, monochrome colour scheme and high-end tech, every bit of it oozed money.

A true billionaires' playground—and it had been a long time since Maria had been surrounded by such wealth. Though even Fraser's wealth as a world-renowned cosmetic surgeon paled in comparison to this.

'You're going to have to close that mouth of yours before we meet and greet,' Trix said with a laugh, shoving open the door to their cabin. 'Mind if I take the bottom bunk?'

She gestured to the beds and Maria swung her case up top. 'No worries.'

'So, you going to tell me what happened after I left the other night?'

Maria rolled her eyes. 'I've only just got on board. Do you wanna help me find my sea legs first before interrogating me?'

Trix chuckled and tossed her a neat stack of clothing. 'Your uniform… So something *did* happen?'

'I admit nothing.'

'Well, while you're admitting "nothing", can you get into the top set—white shirt, navy skirt? They're your whites for greeting the guests. You'll need the blues for daywear, and blacks for evening service.'

'*How* many outfits?'

'You'll be glad of them. It gets hot and dirty on deck.'

Maria cocked a brow. 'Why do you have to make everything sound so X-rated?'

'Hey, it's not the mouth it comes out of, darl…'

'So they say, but in your case they'd definitely make an exception.'

'Enough with the insults.' Trix tossed a pillow at her. 'Do you want this gig or not?'

'Yeah, I want the gig,' she said, stripping out of her travel clothes. 'You want to give me the lowdown on our boss and his guests while I change?'

'On it.' Trix plonked herself on the bottom bunk and ran through the preference sheet on her phone, giving Maria the highlights as she went.

There was the owner of the yacht, a Mr Montgomery. Forty-six. Old money and on the face of it easy to please. Trix loved working for him. Then there were his guests. Two women, of no relation. Twenty-six. Models, with *all* the dietary requirements and *all* the demands. They were going to be a hoot!

But three guests versus an entire bar—it had to be easier, right? And it certainly paid better. And if they were demanding enough to keep her extra busy, her mind would quit trekking back to the very same night Trix wanted to unpack.

And Maria had done enough unpacking this past week to last a lifetime. She did *not* need to go back over it. Verbally, especially.

It was supposed to have been one night of fun, of letting go and living in the moment. Not living in it every moment since. But Tim was proving hard to shift. His smile, his eyes, his warmth and his honesty...*no regrets, remember.*

She tucked the shirt into her navy skirt and turned to face the mirror on the back of their bathroom door, smoothing her hair back into the same functional bun Trix was sporting. 'How do I look?'

'Like you belong here, darl.'

'Attention all crew, attention all crew...' Trix's walkie-talkie crackled to life. 'This is your Captain speaking. Guests are on the dock. I need you all on the aft deck for meet and greet.'

'It's showtime,' Trix said, tossing Maria her

own walkie-talkie to clip to her skirt and launching to her feet. 'You good?'

'I'm good.'

She followed her back upstairs to the grand saloon. 'Grab the face towels from the fridge, won't you? We'll take them out with the champagne.'

'Face towels, on it.'

Trix popped the cork on a bottle and filled three glasses, while Maria arranged the chilled towels into a neat triangle on the tray, topping it off with a fresh flower head from the display beside the bar.

'Nice touch,' Trix said. 'I knew you'd be a natural at this.'

Making things look pretty had been her speciality once upon a time. As a live-in maid in Fraser's household, she'd often been called upon to prettify a room or two. The odd flower on a pillow. A welcome arrangement in the hall. A full-on themed display for a house party.

A flower could lift the plainest of things—they'd made Fraser smile too. And the pleasure she'd got from receiving that simple gesture as a teenager made her recoil in horror now. How stupid she had been. How young and gullible and foolish. Selfish too.

'Hey, it was meant as a compliment.'

Her head snapped up, eyes blinking through the pain of her past to her present and Trix.

'You okay?'

'Sorry, yeah, head elsewhere.'

Which it had been a lot this past week. As if seeing Tim had somehow stirred it all up.

'Well, get it back, you need your game face on.' Trix slid the tray her way. 'Remember, it's just like serving on land with the occasional rock 'n' roll of the water.'

'Easy-peasy,' she said, taking up the tray with a well-practised smile.

'That's the business!'

They joined the receiving line out on the aft deck and Trix quickly introduced her. There was Captain Kali, Chief Engineer Danis, First Officer Russell and Chef Rio. Running back and forth on the gangplank, hauling luggage on board, were Bosun Anya and her number two, Deckhand Bobby.

'Smiles at the ready, folks!' Kali murmured as a trio came into view. A tall blond guy flanked by two women hanging off each arm. One of them raised her shades and gave a little squeal, clapping her hands with glee.

'Oh, God, we've got a squealer,' Trix said under her breath, rousing a giggle from all in earshot.

'Trix…' Kali warned.

'Don't worry, Captain, they can squeal all they like. Their wish is my command.'

'Glad to hear it…'

The sun was already beating down and Maria was grateful for the shade being gifted by the fly-

bridge above. She was used to working indoors—
her lightly freckled skin and the sun didn't mix.
No matter how much she lathered herself in sun-
block.

'Mr Montgomery,' Kali said, stepping forward
as the man himself came up the gangplank. 'Welcome aboard, sir.'

'Hey, Captain!'

The man saluted before shaking Kali's hand. He
was everything Maria had envisaged. Designer
shades atop his foppish blond hair, blue eyes, all
smiles and bronzed skin. His clothes too—chino
shorts and a white polo with a sweater draped
over his shoulders as if he was between tennis
matches, not land and sea. And though he acted
casual enough, men like him, like Fraser, like
Tim, they radiated wealth like the yacht itself.

As for the models, they looked identical save
for their hair colour. Cherry was blonde. Dana,
a dark brunette. Golden tans, oversized shades,
bright white smiles, triangles for bikini tops and
the smallest strips for skirts.

What she couldn't work out was the connection
between models and man? Friends? Associates?
Lovers? She gave a discreet shudder. She hoped
not. He was old enough to be their father.

*Says the girl who fell in love with her boss
twenty years her senior!*

Maybe that was why it turned her stomach
while her smile ached upon her face, her mask

staying in place as Captain ran through the introductions and she held out the tray.

'Towel?' she said smoothly. 'Champagne?'

'Thank you,' Montgomery said, his eyes narrowing on her as he took a swig. 'I've not seen you on board before, you're new?'

'Last-minute addition to the crew,' Trix said for her. 'Sadie's done herself a mischief skiing in Switzerland.'

'Ouch, hope she's okay?'

To his credit, Montgomery looked genuinely concerned.

'Nothing a bit of plaster and bedrest won't fix.'

'Get her some flowers, won't you, Trix?'

Generous too. Then again, with his kind of money, he could afford to be.

'Sure thing.'

'Something big with—' He froze midsentence, his gaze snapping back to the dock as a broad grin spread across his face. 'Well, bugger me, he actually made it.'

'Who made it?' Cherry asked, sipping her champagne and squinting towards the dock.

'Captain, make it a charter for four,' he said over her, slapping his glass back onto Maria's tray before striding towards the gangplank as every eye followed.

Four it is. Maria turned to head inside for extra supplies—then she saw him.

Her breath hitched. Her step faltered. The tray wobbled in her grip.

Tim?

No. It couldn't be.

But it was.

'Ohmigod,' Trix murmured close behind her, 'isn't that—'

'Yes,' Maria said through clenched teeth. 'Yes, it is.'

She watched, frozen in a strange mix of fascination and dread, as Montgomery embraced the man she'd sworn she would never see again.

'Trix,' the captain prompted, glancing their way as neither of them moved. 'We need refreshments for our new guest.'

'On it.' Trix gave her a gentle nudge and Maria tugged her gaze away, forcing her leaden limbs to move.

'Now you're *really* going to have to tell me what happened,' Trix said as soon as they were inside.

She slid the tray onto the counter behind the bar and shook off her trembling fingers. 'What's he doing here, Trix?'

'Damned if I know, he's never been on board before and I've been working *Celeste* for a couple of years now. But Connor has a lot of friends and, judging by that scene out there, I'd say they're pretty close. We'd best get the other stateroom made up.'

'Stateroom?'

'The other master suite.'

'Oh, God, right. Yeah.'

He'd be sleeping on board. For days. For nights.

She'd thought the yacht huge before, now it was nowhere near big enough!

To set sail with the man she had slept with not one week ago…to wait on the man she had slept with…

In the bar, it had been different. They'd been in her domain, it had been on her terms. Here, she was a fish out of water, on a boat with no escape. She'd laugh if it wasn't so messed up.

If Connor and his young guests hadn't put Fraser in her head to begin with, this weird twist of fate surely would have. She couldn't be that person again, sleeping with the man she was supposed to serve…the gossip, the looks, the subservience.

But how could she possibly press reset on their relationship when that ship had already sailed?

'You sly dog!' Connor leapt down the gangplank, his blue eyes as bright as the sky above. 'Making me think you weren't going to show and then rolling up in the nick of time.'

'Sorry, wasn't intentional. A last-minute change of plan.'

Because for the past few days, he'd been fighting the urge to return to a bar in the suburbs—

and to a certain barmaid he couldn't get out of his head. But she'd made her feelings clear. And if he was on a boat at sea there'd be no risk of him going against them.

Hell, he'd probably done enough 'interfering' striking up a deal with her landlord, Mickey, and seeing to it that the building got the work it needed. It was time to move on. And sailing away from temptation made that much easier to do.

'Hey, Connor-baby, you going to introduce us?'

He looked over his friend's shoulder to see one of the young women from the party the other night teetering down the gangplank, closely followed by the other. 'I thought it was just going to be us?'

'What can I say, you bailed, they asked, and I thought what the hell?'

'Right,' he drawled, his frown building. 'In that case, I'll let you get on.' This wasn't the boys' trip he wanted or needed. Throwing his bag over his shoulder, he started to turn away. 'We'll catch up when you're back.'

'Oh, no, you don't.' Connor jumped in his path. 'There's plenty of room for us all and Cherry and Dana are great company. We'll make sure you enjoy yourself, won't we, girls?'

With tinkling laughs, the girls flanked Connor, curling into his side and blocking Tim's exit.

'This is Cherry.' The blonde gave a flutter of

a wave. 'This is Dana.' The brunette blew a kiss. 'Girls, this is my friend, Campbell.'

'Hi, Campbell,' they cooed.

'Hi,' he said, his smile strained. 'But despite what Connor just said, I'm heading off. Look after him out there, won't you?'

Cherry jutted out her bottom lip. 'You're not going to stay?'

'Please say you'll stay,' Dana said with her, perfecting the same pout.

'As much as I'd love to...' He wouldn't. He'd rather stick pins in his eyes than play third wheel to this trio. But he didn't want to offend them any more than his quick exit already would. 'I'm afraid I'm going to have to take a raincheck.'

'Come on, Tim.' Connor's easy demeanour shifted into concern. 'You need this break.'

'You're not leaving because of us, are you?' Cherry purred, blue eyes blinking rapidly. 'Because that'll make us feel bad.'

'And you don't want to make us feel bad, do you?' Dana added in the same pleading tone.

My God, had Connor *paid* them to do this? Though it wasn't their eyes he saw now, it was Sasha's. His daughter pleading with him to get a life again. But this wasn't the kind of life he wanted any part of. It might work for Connor, but it didn't work for him.

'Nothing to do with you ladies, I can assure you.'

His friend cursed under his breath. 'Can you give us a moment, ladies?'

'Of course,' Dana said, peeling herself away.

'Just don't be too long,' Cherry murmured. 'That yacht's too big for the two of us. Not to mention the beds...'

They sashayed their way back on deck and Tim forked a hand through his hair. 'Don't you get tired of it?'

'Tired of what?'

'The meaningless hook-ups?'

Because yes, he'd hooked up with Maria, but it had felt far from meaningless.

'Those girls are fun, serious fun. And before you say anything else about me being old enough to be their father, at least they don't make me feel twice my age, which is what you do when you're being all...' He waved a hand at him.

'All what? Mature? Sensible? Need I go on?'

'Look, I just want my old mate back, the guy who laughed easily, smiled even. Is that so much to ask?'

'I'm all for a bit of fun. I just wasn't expecting...' He gestured towards the boat and the two girls giggling on board.

'I'm telling you, they're fun.'

'To you maybe. I prefer my women a little more...'

Words failed him as Maria launched to the forefront of his mind for the umpteenth time...the stewardess now serving the girls a fresh glass of champagne making him think of her too. He could only see her from behind, but her hair bore the same caramel streaks as Maria. And there was something about the way she held herself too.

Great! Now he was *seeing* her everywhere. He really did have it bad.

'See! You can't even remember what you like, it's been that long.'

'That isn't true,' he said, dragging his eyes back to Connor's. 'I just know they're not it. I honestly think you'll have a much better time without me.'

'You know what your problem is, you *think* too much these days. It's eat, sleep, work, repeat, and it's time to break free of the cycle. You used to love getting out on the open water. *We* used to love getting out together,' his friend reiterated.

'That was before.'

'*Everything* was before in your world, but it's all still here for the taking. And the sun is shining, the sea is calling, so no more thought, no more work, no more worries, yeah. And it'll make Sasha happy too.'

'You need to stop conspiring with my daughter.'

'Who says we're conspiring?'

'I do. It's why you invited me, is it not? Some kind of intervention to get me out of this perceived rut I'm in.'

'Intervention?' Connor chuckled. 'If you want

to see it that way. I prefer to see it as a long over-due boys' trip.'

'And the women?'

'A healthy addition. But you can leave them to me and get out on the water, get some diving in, if you want, spend time with the fish if you prefer their company to ours. We won't be offended.'

'You're really selling it.'

He grinned. 'I know. When was the last time you scuba dived?'

'Too long to be doing it again now without a refresher.'

'And what the hell is that about? You *loved* diving! And you always squeezed in a trip to Gabo Island when you could.'

Ellie. It was all about Ellie and the fact that she had loved it too. And enjoying the same stuff without Ellie only made her absence all the more pronounced.

'Don't you think you owe it to her?'

It was as if his friend was in his head, reading his very thoughts…

'Sasha gets enough out of me,' he said, deliberately misunderstanding him.

'I meant Ellie.'

'I know who you meant.'

'You just didn't want to acknowledge her.'

'That's not…' He rubbed the back of his neck, giving up on the lie.

'You know, the more you talk about something the less power it has to hurt you.'

He'd fight back if not for the fact that Connor knew it from experience. He'd lost his entire family at the age of twenty-one—mother, father, sister, brother, all gone in a road traffic accident. Overnight, he'd become one of the wealthiest men alive, and the loneliest.

And no matter what Connor said about facing it and moving on, Tim was convinced his friend ran from his past daily. Hence the parties, the yachts, the girls...*everything* was fun in Connor's world.

But saying it was fun didn't automatically make it so.

'Tim, I'm serious. She was the one who died, not you. You owe it to her to live your life for the two of you.'

'And is that what you're still doing, living it for the five of you?'

Connor's lashes flickered, his blue eyes flashed. Shit.

'I'm sorry, mate, I shouldn't have.'

'No, I'll own it. And so what if I am?' he threw back. 'It beats the alternative half-life you seem to insist on living.' He looked to the boat and sighed. 'Look, if you truly hate it after one night, you can send for the chopper...or we can evict the chicks. Bros before—'

'Connor, so help me, if you finish that phrase.'

'But you know what I'm saying.'

'I do.'

He glanced at the yacht just as the stewardess with the champagne turned and his body jolted. *Maria?*

The crew uniform dulled her individuality, but he'd know her anywhere. The high cheekbones, the soft arch of her brows, the quiet intensity of those almond-shaped eyes. And that mouth…full, teasing, the faintest tilt at the corners.

My God, it really was her.

'See,' Connor said, 'she has a glass of champagne with your name on.'

His head wasn't playing tricks on him. She was here. On Connor's yacht. Questions raced as fast as his feet—*How? What? When? Why?*

'Best not keep her waiting any longer then…'

'You're *coming*?' Connor said, hurrying after him.

Another stewardess approached the rail and he did a double-take—the other barmaid! *She* was on board *too*. A hell of a coincidence. Or fate.

Either way, he was wholeheartedly on board with it.

'It's going to be great,' Connor said, full of cheer again. 'I promise.'

But the only person capable of making good on that promise was the woman staring back at him…her eyes getting wider by the second.

CHAPTER SIX

MARIA'S PULSE TRIPPED—one minute the two men were in deep debate on the dock, the next Tim was closing in at pace, Montgomery hot on his tail.

Just breathe.

Breathe and smile.

She backed up when he stepped onto the deck, his familiar grey eyes more dazzling than the sun. Especially when they shone with such joy at her presence. 'What are you—'

She stiffened, her eyes flaring, urging him to stop.

Don't out me. Don't out us!

Heat flushed her cheeks as every gaze on deck turned their way and he frowned, clearly trying to make sense of her reaction.

Wasn't it obvious? She didn't want the crew to know they knew each other. Worse still, that they'd slept together!

Not that one automatically led to the other, but...

'What are you—what?' Montgomery cut in,

coming up alongside him and taking a fresh drink from her tray.

'What are you serving?' Tim said smoothly, following her cue. But her stunned brain lagged, too slow to answer.

'Bolly, of course!' Montgomery clasped Tim's shoulder. 'Now, grab yourself one and I'll introduce you to the crew.'

He reached for a glass, his intense gaze burning with a thousand questions, not that she was about to answer any. She kept her smile steady, but inside…inside *everything* raced. Her heart. Her pulse. Her mind.

'This is Maria,' Montgomery said.

He nodded. 'Maria.'

The memory of him saying the very same against her ear made her shiver. Her body reliving it and all the rest. Eager to remember…and reacquaint herself all over.

'Welcome aboard, Mr Campbell.' *Damn.* Was it the blood in her ears or did her voice really sound that thick? 'Towel?'

His mouth twitched. 'Do I look in need of one?'

She wet her lips as heat fractured right through her. He looked hot. So hot. And he knew it. His eyes sparked back at her, daring her to say it too.

'No.' She swallowed, feeding off his provocation to regain the fight. 'You look perfectly refreshed.'

Montgomery was watching their exchange with

interest—hell, the entire crew were! She turned away before her mask could slip any more and Montgomery continued with the introductions. Though her eyes wouldn't be told, they kept drifting his way. Hungry for more.

He looked good in the sun. The deep grey polo shirt and pale grey shorts working with the grey of his eyes, his salt-and-pepper hair, his lightly bronzed skin...

And here she was, plain Jane. Her own style swapped out for the uniform of the yacht. The single stripe to each shoulder denoting her first stew, bottom-rung status. Whereas he was very much top rung and then some.

He caught her eye and she glanced away, ears ringing, cheeks burning, her heart beating too hard and too fast...

'Is that all of your luggage, sir?' Trix asked him as soon as the introductions were over.

Maria couldn't blame her friend for checking. Not when the others had brought a series of cases on board, most of them large enough to house the possessions of an entire family.

'It is.'

'Wonderful. If you just leave it here, Maria can unpack it while I take you for a tour of the yacht and the facilities.'

'A tour?' Cherry giggled. 'Is that really necessary?'

'You'll want to know how everything works,'

Trix explained while Maria's heart did cartwheels at the idea of being in his room, unpacking his things, even without him there. 'Especially the spa pool and the dancefloor.'

'Oh, yes!' Dana hooked her arm through Cherry's. 'Show us the way.'

Trix sent Maria a look that said *Wish me luck* and started to guide them away.

'Actually,' Tim said, 'do you mind if I come with you, Maria?'

She gave a startled, 'Huh!', her jaw snapping back together so tight she swore she felt a tooth crack.

'Don't mind, do you, Connor?' he said, hoisting his bag onto his shoulder. 'I could do with making a few calls before signing off.'

Montgomery paused at the stairs to the flybridge as Trix led the girls up. 'No worries, just make sure you leave your phone down there, yeah? Boys' trip, remember!'

Maria's stomach clenched. Boys' trip? Wasn't that code for... Her eyes lifted to the flybridge above, to where the two girls were now cooing over Montgomery joining them. Was one for him and one for... Her eyes returned to Tim, her heart jerking as he gave the smallest shake of his head. Was she that obvious?

And hell, she wasn't jealous. She had no right to be jealous. She didn't care.

Only she did.

'Mr Campbell,' Captain Kali said, snagging his attention, 'I'll leave you in Maria's capable hands. I'm sure you'll find everything to your satisfaction but any problems, please don't hesitate to let us know.'

'I'm sure everything will be just fine.' His gaze flitted her way, like she had some say in it. 'Thanks, Captain.'

Everyone dispersed. They were alone. And she couldn't feel the tray in her hands any more, couldn't feel the warm wood beneath her feet either. Her senses were all about him. His scent, his heat, his proximity...

'Do you want to come this way?' she said, belatedly remembering her role and what she was *supposed* to be doing—showing him to his room—not *actually* doing—ogling him.

Trix had pointed out the second master stateroom, but she had no clue what awaited beyond the door.

She would get in and out as quickly as possible. Stock up the supplies, unpack his case, make the bed. *The bed.* She gulped as she pushed her way through the saloon, leaving the tray on the bar as she went.

'I don't think your room is made up yet. It shouldn't take me too long to have it ready for you though.'

She didn't look back as she said it. Didn't pause either as she hit the stairs. It was hard not to appear as if she was running from him but everything about this situation had her screaming to do just that.

'You don't need to panic.' He sounded amused— or was that bemused? 'I've seen an unmade bed before.'

It wasn't the *state* of the bed she was panicking about.

All around her, the shiny grandeur of the yacht had her feeling ever more out of place. As for his presence now in it... She'd known he was money. In the bar, she'd known. But here, now, with their roles on board accentuating their differences... It was hard to believe that less than a week ago he'd been in her bar, in *her* bed, making her forget her worries and her strife—and now she sounded like freaking Baloo in *The Jungle Book*!

What was wrong with her?

'Maria...?'

Him! He was what was wrong, her body pulsing over her name on his lips like it was everything she needed to hear when it wasn't.

'This is you,' she said, pushing open his door and losing herself in the showy display ahead because losing herself in him was *not* an option.

He walked ahead of her, his tall, broad frame a tiny blip in the room that seemed to extend forever. The colour palette was softer here, the muted greys and whites soothing on the eye, the accent lighting too. As for the panoramic view of the open sea, breathtaking.

She couldn't imagine wanting anything else. Not when every need was catered for. Space to eat, space to work, space to bathe, to relax, to… sleep. The giant bed, floating on an illuminated platform in the heart of the room, was already made up, its crisp white bedding like an inviting cloud calling out to be…

'Looks like your room is made up already,' she blurted, snapping her gaze away.

'So it is.'

He showed no sign of sharing her stress as he tossed his bag on the tempting cloud.

Just her then. Great.

'If you let me know when you're done with your calls, I'll come back and sort the rest.'

She was on the threshold when he came upon her. 'Wait!'

She blinked up at him, surprised by his sudden shift, surprised even more by his sudden proximity. She forced her face to relax, aiming for polite indifference, probably achieving lemon-sucking standard if his furrowed brow was anything to go by.

God, this was hard! She'd never needed to *feign* politeness in the bar, but here, on a superyacht, it was all change. In every way. 'Yes?'

'I don't have calls to make.'

'No?'

'I wanted to talk to you.'

Of course you did... 'About?'

'Isn't it obvious?'

She took a breath. Time to lay some ground rules. 'Look, Mr Campbell—'

He flinched. *'Just* Tim. Please.'

The smallest huff escaped. 'I'm afraid that's above my pay grade.'

'Seriously? After everything we shared the other night, you think I'm going to be okay with you addressing me in that way?'

She stiffened, glancing down the hallway. Thank God, it was empty.

'Things were different then,' she said under her breath. 'You weren't my boss for a start.'

'I'm not your boss now.'

'You might as well be.'

He raked a hand through his hair, took another step towards her. 'I don't need waiting on by you. By anyone. I'm more than capable of unpacking my own case, fetching my own drinks—'

'You going to cook your own dinner too, because Chef Rio won't like that.'

'Maria, please...'

'What?' She gave an awkward laugh, trying desperately to make light of a situation that was anything but. 'It sounds like you want to put us out of work.'

And she didn't care if she sounded extreme. Her job on board was to serve, and serving them well could see her earning a tip worth more than a month's wage at the bar. Not that he could even begin to understand that, so she had to be the one to make it clear to him.

'This job is important to me. Please don't make it any more awkward than it already is.'

'I'm not. Or at least I'm trying not to. But having you run around after me...it's not right.'

'It's perfectly fine,' she assured him as smoothly as she could. 'This is my job.' *Now draw the line and don't cross it.* 'What we shared the other night is in the past and I'd like for us to keep it that way.'

'You don't want anyone to know we slept together?'

'Of course I don't!'

Too loud, Maria.

'Why? Are you ashamed of me?'

'Ashamed? God, no.'

'Good. Because, the way I see it, we were two consenting adults, getting to know one another and having a good time. At least, I thought that was the case and now we're here—'

'That *was* the case.'

She wasn't about to lie about that.

'Then why on earth pretend we've never met?'

'Because I don't want it getting out.'

'Why?'

'Because on this yacht I'm the crew, you're a guest, we don't mix.'

'We more than mixed.'

'Tim!'

His mouth quirked to one side. 'At least you're calling me Tim now.'

Heat bloomed in her cheeks and her chest and her belly…but she refused to bow down. 'This isn't funny.'

'You think I think it is? You're out there wanting me to pretend nothing happened between us, that I don't even know you, when I know *every* inch of you.'

She cursed, her, 'Yes!' a panicked hiss.

'But that friend of yours, the other stewardess, she was working with you in the bar the other night, wasn't she? She knows we know each other.'

'She knows you were there having a drink. She doesn't know what came after.'

'Right. So what am I to be, your dirty little secret for the next few days because I—what? What did I say?'

She knew she was pale, her past draining the blood from her face, but she'd been the dirty little secret, her daughter Fae even more so… Tim could give himself the label all he liked, but his superior status would forever ensure he was on the right side of that equation.

'Maria? What is—'

'I need to go. Like I said, let me know when you're finished in your room, and I'll take care of your things. Or Trix will, if that makes you more comfortable.'

It would certainly be Maria's preference.

And then she legged it, before she went back on every word, every warning, and acted on the chemistry threatening to break her. But how long could she resist when they were on a boat in the middle of the ocean together and he wanted to...?

He wanted to what? She hadn't let him finish. She'd been too scared of what he would say. Too scared he'd see this weird twist of fate as a reason to extend their one night into several...and the idea of that...the temptation—gah!

Some flamin' pickle to be in when there was no way out of the freaking jar.

Tim stared at the door as it clicked shut. She didn't slam it. No, that would be too unprofessional, and she was being professional to a fault.

Hell, he could understand her need to set them both apart. To keep her place amongst the crew. But he'd never had to lie about knowing someone before and it didn't sit right. Especially when he got the impression that something else was amiss. Something that had nothing to do with him and everything to do with her.

His phone buzzed in his pocket and he pulled it out, glanced at the screen: Sasha.

Happy sailing, Dad! Enjoy it! Xxx

How did she— Connor! He shook his head and sent a reply:

Thank you. You can stop keeping tabs on me now x

Never. LOL x

He laughed softly. This was *not* how it should be. A daughter keeping a close eye on her father. Worrying about her father. It was time to show her he was good. That life was good. Even if he didn't truly feel it.

Though a week ago…a week ago it had shone with possibility again.

All because of a woman, and that in itself was a problem.

His happiness had once centred on Ellie and look how bereft that had left him.

He should be grateful to Maria for seeing sense when he couldn't. Keeping him at arm's length was as good for him as it was for her.

Even if it went against his every instinct…

'Everything okay?'

Trix was mixing drinks in the saloon when Maria came up a short while later.

'Yup.' Though she couldn't look at Trix as she said it. 'The room's already made up, but I said I'd sort his stuff once he was done.'

'I wasn't referring to the room.'

Maria's Spidey-senses tingled… 'Hmm?'

'He *is* the guy from the bar the other night, right?'

She nodded, taking up a sofa cushion and fluffing it with more focus than it needed.

'Of all the bars in all the world,' she murmured, 'and all the yachts in the sea…'

'Yeah, yeah, I know.'

'You think it's the universe trying to tell you something?'

'Like what, Trix?' She threw the cushion down and met her friend's sparkling brown gaze. 'Hey, Maria, here's that guy again, you know, the one you liked, now go serve him while he enjoys the company of two women a thousand times more beautiful and at home in his world. How's that for fun?'

Her friend laughed. 'Are you for real? Did you not *see* the way he was checking you out again?'

'I think he was in shock.'

Liar.

'Na-ah, those were full-on puppy-dog eyes out there. And if I had a rich widower taking a shine to me, I wouldn't be denying all knowledge of him. What was that about, anyway?'

'I don't want the crew thinking we…thinking there's something going on between us,' she said, swiftly adding, 'when there very much *isn't.*'

'And you think people knowing you've met before would give them the wrong idea?'

She shrugged. 'I don't know. Maybe.'

'Do you not think you're being an itty-bit paranoid?'

She didn't answer.

'There are plenty of *innocent* ways you could have met, the bar included, and no one would have thought it strange. Strikes me as your guilty conscience talking...'

Maria pressed her lips together.

'Something *did* happen, didn't it? That's why you're acting all kooky?'

Her teeth ground together.

'I *knew* it.'

'Trix, please, I don't want to make a huge deal of it. And I really don't want the crew finding out.'

'No one's gonna hear it from me, I promise you that. Good on you for finally getting some fun in!'

'And look where it's landed me.'

'It's hardly the end of the world.'

'You might not mind running around after a guy you had *sex* with,' she said under her breath. 'But it freaks me out.'

'Feels like a good excuse for some cheeky role play, if you ask me.'

'I didn't ask.'

And now her gut was rolling because *that* kind of role play had once been her life. For better or for worse. Memories she didn't want to face playing out in blazing Technicolor as the sickness welled.

She turned away before Trix could notice her pallor, busied herself rearranging the flower display on the bar.

'Sorry, darl, I was just teasing.'

'I know.'

Though Trix wouldn't have said it if she knew her story. If she knew who Fae's father was. But no one knew that sordid tale, except for Fae and the man himself. The staff had suspected enough and made her life hell. Never Fraser's though, because that had been more than their jobs' worth.

'It really isn't all that bad, you know. All sorts happen on these yachts.'

'You saying it wouldn't bother you at all?' she said quietly. 'A stew carrying on with a guest?'

'Of course it would, but this is different.'

'How?'

'You weren't my stew on land, for a start.'

'And now I am?'

'Before you turned ghost like, I was just happy to see you glowing.'

'Glowing?' she blustered. 'That's ridiculous.'

'You clearly haven't looked in the mirror lately.'

Actually, she had. And she knew Trix was right. He'd lit a spark within her, and now she couldn't put the damn thing out.

'All I'm saying is, don't be so quick to dismiss

it. Especially when he appears to be one of the good ones.'

'The good ones…?'

'I've never seen a guest carry his own bags before.'

'He had one, Trix. One!'

'Yeah, not seen that before either. A wealthy man that travels light, a rare breed indeed. You really do need to lock him down.'

'Enough! Tell me what you want me to do next…and keep it clean!'

Trix pursed her lips to the side, her eyes dancing. 'Okay, spoilsport. The lads have taken all the bags down. You okay to tackle Cherry and Dana's room while I keep the drinks flowing?'

'Sure.'

It would also give her a good hour or so tucked away from Tim.

Out of sight, out of mind.

She could hope…

CHAPTER SEVEN

HOURS LATER, TIM was trying to relax in a lounger on the upper deck. He had a book in one hand, a soda and lime in the other and, on the face of it, looked to be having an idyllic afternoon beside the pool.

They were due to anchor in Refuge Cove for the night before continuing on to Gabo Island come morning. Weather conditions along the Bass Strait were good. Smooth sailing all the way. What more could one want?

Not the question to ask when it had been hours since he'd last set eyes on Maria. And the idea that she was avoiding him had him all at sea— *at sea?* Great. Even his conscience was having a laugh at his expense.

A squeal from Dana pierced his eardrums and he peered over the edge of his book.

She was reclining along the water's edge, supposedly sunbathing, with every curve angled just so. While Cherry was splashing about with Connor in the water.

It was the splashing that had Dana squealing.

'I'm going to have to wash my hair before dinner now, you pair of beasts,' she admonished, shaking out her ponytail and resuming her position.

'You were going to wash it anyway, darling,' Cherry said. 'Be honest.'

'I suppose I was.'

'But, speaking of dinner...' Cherry hooked her arms and legs around Connor. 'Shouldn't we be getting ready?'

'Ready? It's at least two hours away,' Connor said. 'And we're not going anywhere but the aft deck, so bikinis are perfectly acceptable.'

'You'd like that, wouldn't you?' Cherry rocked in his arms, her body moving in tune with the low, sultry beats coming through the sound system.

'What man wouldn't?' Connor said, nuzzling into her neck and making her moan unashamedly.

Tim rolled his eyes and leaned back. If this was how it was going to go, maybe he—

Movement to his right caught his eye. Caramel hair, lightly sunkissed skin, pale blue polo, navy shorts and a whole lot of leg—Maria!

Any thought of jumping ship swiftly quit.

'Three Sex on the Beach?' she called out, lifting the tray of colourful cocktails and carefully avoiding his eye.

'Perfect timing,' Connor said. 'Trix work her special magic with them?'

'An added twist of coconut?'

'That's the one.'

'Sounds divine,' Dana murmured, getting to her feet and stretching out her body in the barely-there bikini. Tim didn't know where to look. And from the way Maria glanced his way, she didn't either. He gave her the smallest of smiles, which she *almost* returned, then Dana swept between them, pulling on her sheer robe and taking up a glass.

'Thank you, sweetheart.'

Maria's smile tightened. 'You're welcome.'

'Time to get ready—you coming, Cherry?'

'Not yet she isn't,' Connor said, shamelessly nuzzling her neck still, 'but give us a minute.'

For the love of...

Tim closed his book. Not even the chill of a good thriller could distract from Connor in full-on playboy mode. 'There will be nothing left of her to get ready if you keep that up.'

'Promises, promises,' Cherry cooed, easing out of Connor's grasp and pushing up out of the pool. If Dana's bikini was barely-there, Cherry's might as well not exist, the white fabric having turned transparent with the water. Not that Connor or Cherry seemed to mind the design flaw.

She took her cocktail from the tray as her gaze found Tim's and she smiled around her straw. 'You want to swap that soda for one of these, baby, and come join us below deck?'

Tim exhaled slowly. 'I'm good, thanks.'

'Party-pooper,' Cherry pouted.

'Am I not enough for you?' Connor said, easing out of the water too, his rash vest clinging to his torso. His clothed state at total odds with the company he was keeping, but then, Tim knew what that vest hid. Scars that ran deeper than just the surface.

'You're always enough, darling.' Cherry trailed a hand down Connor's front as he wrapped a towel around her shoulders and drew her close. 'But your friend looks like he could do with cheering up and we're nothing if not cheer-inducing.'

Maria made a noise which she quickly masked with a cough, her averted gaze catching Tim's again. His mouth twitched with hers. The laughter in her hazel depths unmistakable.

'Can I get you something else?' she asked, finally sparing him more than a glance as she gestured to his glass.

'What's on offer?' And then he cringed as Maria blushed and Connor chortled. In any normal situation, that question would have been perfectly innocent. But hot off the back of the trio's antics… 'I meant drinks—what drinks do you have?'

'Sure you did, buddy,' Connor said, urging Cherry towards the stairs. 'And you know my yacht is as well stocked as any bar on land when it comes to drinks of your variety. Come on, ladies, let's leave Tim to dig himself out of that hole while we go get ready. Maybe he can find his funny bone while he's down there.'

'Remind me why we're friends again,' he muttered after him.

'You love me really.'

'Yeah, yeah…'

'If you change your mind…' Dana said, trailing her hand across Tim's bare shoulder before slinking off down the stairs behind them.

He rubbed away the goosebumps she'd fired up and dragged his gaze back to Maria's. The tightness around her eyes putting a fire under him as he launched to his feet. 'I'm so sorry about that.'

She gave a flustered laugh. 'You don't need to apologise.'

'Oh, I do, and I fear it won't be the last time either.'

He threw back the last of his soda water, but it did nothing to quench his thirst. Not when every inch of his body wanted to reacquaint itself with hers. Not helped by the fact that he was half-naked.

He raked a hand through his hair and her eyes dipped to his chest, colour surging to her cheeks before they snapped back to his. What he wouldn't give to act on that heat…

'Sometimes I think he shouldn't be let out in public.'

Now she laughed, a true easy tinkle that warmed

and relaxed every tightened muscle. 'I've met worse.' Then she nipped her lip as her eyes flared. 'And I shouldn't have said that.'

'Don't worry, I won't tell if you won't.'

She met his smile curve for curve, her eyes warming as she blinked up at him. 'How did you two become friends? You don't seem anything alike.'

'We were at boarding school together. He was a couple of years below me, but we played sport together. Hit it off. He's more of a brother than a mate.'

'Is that why you tolerate him?'

He chuckled. 'He's really not so bad once you get beneath all the bluster.'

'No?'

'We actually used to be quite similar.'

'Is that so?'

'Could barely tell us apart…'

She arched one brow, her eyes dancing. 'Like Tweedledee and Tweedledum?'

'Something like that.'

'So…' she lifted the empty tray to her chest '…what happened?'

Ah, so much for easy…

'Life.'

'That old chestnut, hey?' Then her smile faded with his. 'Sorry, that was really crass. Your wife…' She ran a hand over her smoothed back hair. 'Forgive me, I should go.'

She moved off and he intercepted her, gripping the handrail to stop himself from reaching for her. 'You have nothing to apologise for either.'

Her gaze lifted to his, guilt still shining in her eyes as her lips softly parted. And he couldn't look at them when he was trying to tell her this.

'Losing her did change me.' He turned to face the sea, watching as the sun slowly dipped behind the horizon. 'Most would say not for the better, too. Connor was no different...'

'Connor was married?'

'No. God, no. Connor can't imagine anything worse than giving himself to someone in that way. To love someone. Crazy thing is, he does still love. He loves me. He loves Sasha. He loved Ellie.' He gave Maria the smallest smile.

'Who did he lose?'

'His entire family.'

She gasped softly and he gave a slow nod. 'He was the only one to walk away from their car after a lorry sideswiped it on the motorway. Mother, father, sister, brother. All gone.'

'Oh, my God. That's awful.'

'He was twenty-one. Too young. He lost himself in his grief for a while and then, when he came out of it, he took the whole "life's too short" motto to a whole other level. There's no such thing as too much fun and there's no time to settle. He won't be tied down, to anyone or to anything. He's very careful about that.'

'So the women?'

'Are as committed to having fun and enjoying the single life as he is.'

Her brows knitted together. 'And what about you?' She turned to lean back against the rail. 'I assume from all the noise, he's hoping you and Dana might…hell, even Cherry…they all seem rather open to sharing.'

He angled his body to face her, his eyes reading every outward sign she dared to give. 'Would it bother you if I did?'

How had she gone from keeping him out of sight, out of mind to this…?

Maria opened her mouth to lie and his brows nudged north, his grey eyes searing her with their honesty, and she couldn't do it.

'Now you're just avoiding the question,' she hedged.

'*I'm* avoiding the question?'

'Yes.'

She took a breath, trying to regain her common sense, but instead she caught his scent. Oh-so familiar to her senses. Deep, spicy and inviting.

She turned to drag in the ocean air instead, willing it to soothe away the excited flurry within.

'I went through a phase,' he admitted, his voice low and gravel-like.

'A phase?' she murmured, resisting the urge to glance his way when it was all her eyes wanted to do. To drink him in up close. To study those eyes that gave away so much and those lips that succeeded in teasing her with words alone.

'I guess you could call it phases, plural.' He rested his forearms on the rail and looked to the sea with her. 'When I first lost Ellie, I couldn't bear being in company. I wanted to be there for my daughter but there were days when even she would tip me over the edge. She looks like her, acts like her... I'd catch sight of her at times and do a double-take before remembering all over again.'

She inhaled softly, her heart aching for him. 'That's hard. But it's something to cherish, having so much of her mother in her.'

'I know that now. I guess I knew that then too, but some days it was just too hard. I was bitter, angry, and I struggled to see past that. Life lost its reason. I'd worked so hard to get to where we were in life, to have all this money, and not be able to save her...to get her prognosis and know there was nothing I could do. Having to be strong when all I wanted to do was scream, *Why her? Why us?*'

'Why anyone?' she murmured, thinking of all those without the money, the connections, who suffered the same fate.

'Precisely. Those were Sasha's words too when she told me she wanted my support to set up a charity in memory of Ellie. She was only nineteen and full of all these incredible ideas. Bursting with them. She ploughed her grief into a venture designed to help others, save others, and I couldn't have been prouder.'

'She sounds amazing.'

'She is. She's an inspiration, not just to me but so many others. And there was a time when I saw that strength in her and realised she didn't need me to provide it any more. I found myself without any real purpose and Connor was there, coaxing me back into the land of the living.'

'Let me guess, then came the phase?'

'Yeah.' He rocked back, looking to the ground as he gave a brusque, bashful laugh. 'It didn't last long, much to Connor's dismay. I think he was happy having a wingman again. Different cities, different women, but I don't know...' he lifted his gaze to the setting sun once more, a crease forming between his brows '...it felt...soulless.'

'Soulless?'

'Yeah.' A small smile played about his lips. 'To be honest, I figured Ellie had ruined me for other women. And then I met you...'

He looked at her, his eyes awash with his words, an emotion she couldn't—*wouldn't* trust.

'Me?'

He gave the smallest nod. 'And for the first time since Ellie, I wanted...'

She swallowed as he turned to her. 'You wanted...?'

The entire world fell away as she lost herself in his eyes...the yacht, the sea, the reality of who they were and what they could never be. She'd blame the dreamlike quality of the sky, its soft pink hue as it turned the sea to liquid gold, but it was all him. Him and his words and his eyes that were all too captivating.

'I wanted you, Maria.' Slowly, he raised a hand to sweep an errant strand behind her ear, his gaze following the move and setting off a gazillion flutters in her chest. 'I still really want you.'

'You shouldn't.'

There were a thousand reasons why he shouldn't. Reasons she could throw at him now, reasons she *should* throw at him. But she was struggling to string a coherent thought together as the fire in the sky spread to his eyes and through her middle.

'It's true.' His hand came to rest beneath her chin, his eyes on her lips. 'I don't want the pain of losing someone I love again. But I can't deny what I feel for you.'

A rush of desire and something far more potent rose up within her, causing her lips to part and her pulse to race.

I want you too... The words were there, pushing at the line she'd sworn she wouldn't cross.

'And I'm not ready to walk away from this. Are you?'

Yes. She had to. She couldn't be that woman

again. Hoodwinked by a man. Ridiculed by her peers. Feeling like a puppet controlled by her feelings. But she couldn't find her feet to walk.

Then he kissed her and she melted. It was the briefest sip against her lips, the lightest sweep of his tongue, and *oh, my God,* she wanted more. So much more.

His lashes lifted, his eyes connecting with hers. 'Maria…?'

The soft sound teased at the protective wall around her heart, hurting and healing and confusing as hell.

'I wish you wouldn't say it like that.'

'Like what?'

Like it was the most beautiful name in the world. A pleasure-filled sigh. A whispered caress along her skin. She gave the smallest shiver as he traced her lower lip with his thumb.

'Like I'm yours,' she whispered. Because to be his…to be loved like he had loved his wife. To be worthy of that kind of love from a man who cared so deeply, felt so deeply…

'I don't mean to. But I am trying to be honest with you.'

'You don't even know me.'

'I know enough. I know how you make me feel. I know I want to know more.'

'No, you don't.'

Because if he knew more, he'd know about Fraser. He'd know she'd betrayed another woman in the worst possible way. He'd know she'd almost torn apart a family and for what...to be a man's mistress, the dirty little secret, the money-grabbing whore to the select few who thought they knew.

Stay in your own flamin' lane, Maria!

'I can't do this.'

She pushed him away, running...

'Maria!'

He was hot on her tail and she spun to face him, hands raised to ward him off as her unshed tears blurred him and the sky into a kaleidoscope of colour.

'Please let it go. I don't deserve your attention. I don't *want* your attention. Just leave it alone.'

And then she fled.

CHAPTER EIGHT

TIM FELT LIKE a jerk. A complete and utter jerk.

She'd made her thoughts clear and then he'd pressed her to the point that she'd felt she'd had no choice but to run. Literally, run. From *him*.

Again.

He'd messed up. Big time. If only he could get her alone, explain, apologise properly...but getting her alone was a problem. He couldn't single her out for a private conversation. That would only arouse suspicion and get her back up more. And trying to catch her alone 'by chance' was proving impossible.

There was always someone else around, and he got the distinct impression she was working hard to make it so. Which only served to make him feel worse.

'It's not often that I admit to being wrong,' Connor said from his lounged back position on the aft deck sofa, making the most of the post-dinner entertainment in the form of Cherry and Dana dancing to some cringe-inducing tune across the way. 'But in this case, I think I might be.'

'Wrong?' Tim frowned. 'About what?'

'You. This trip.' Connor waved his whisky glass at their surroundings, gave Cherry a subtle wink as she caught his eye, and then his gaze landed on Tim, the sudden gravity in its depths piling extra weight on the guilt Tim was already carrying. 'It being good for you.'

'It *is* good for me.'

He raised one lazy brow. 'Yeah, it looks it too.'

'Just ignore me.'

'How can I? You spent the entire dinner acting like your cat just died.'

'I don't have a cat.'

'Maybe you should—it might encourage you to talk more.'

'A *cat*?' He gestured to his friend's drink. 'I think you've had a few too many of those.'

'Na-ah. There was a time we couldn't get you to shut up. Now it's like pulling teeth.'

'And you think a cat is the answer?'

'Desperate times call for desperate measures.'

Tim sipped his whisky, thinking how funny his closest friend should be saying all this when he'd been more than willing to talk a week ago. More than willing to a few hours ago too. Because when he was with Maria everything came alive, his body, his mind…his tongue.

'Glad you find it so amusing,' Connor said.

'I didn't say I found it amusing.'

'The look on your face says otherwise...'

That was what a certain moment with a certain brunette could do. But then he remembered all that came after. The way she'd run...what she'd said...the tears.

'So, you going to tell me what has you so distracted you didn't engage in any of the conversation over dinner?'

'The *conversation*?' Every time he'd risen above the mental replay of his chat with Maria to tune into the talk at the table it had been nothing but ego-stroking nonsense. 'Excuse me if I didn't feel the need to tell you that your efforts in the gym are paying off,' he murmured around his glass, taking a satisfying swig and sending Connor a smile laden with tease. 'Or that your shirt matches your eyes...which it does, by the way.'

Connor laughed and tossed a stray flower head from the table arrangement at his chest. 'All right, I guess I deserved that.' And then he leaned in, resting his elbow on the sofa between them. 'But I'm serious—you going to tell me what's going on in that head of yours?'

'You don't need to know.'

'I kind of feel like I do.'

Something about the way he said it had Tim's back stiffening. 'Why?'

'You're my brother in all the ways that matter for a start.' His friend threw back his drink and gestured to a hovering Trix on the other side of the saloon doors, but it was Maria who stepped out. And no matter that he'd seen her plenty this evening as she'd helped with the dinner service, she still had the power to make his skin fizz with awareness, his body tighten and pulse race.

She wore black tonight, a simple dress that skimmed her knees, but the way the fabric clung to her curves and set off the natural glow to her skin…it hadn't been Chef Rio's food that had had his mouth watering all evening.

'Another whisky for bed, please, Maria. And whatever the girls would like too, of course.'

'We're going to bed?' Cherry said.

'Already?' Dana blurted.

'I figured the three of us could continue this downstairs,' Connor said.

'In that case—' Cherry cracked a grin '—espresso martini, please, Maria.'

'Make that two,' Dana said. 'Gotta keep our energy up.'

Both women threw Connor a coy smile as Maria nodded and swept back inside. She didn't look at Tim. Not once. The story of the entire evening, and the reason for his mood too.

'I saw you two earlier,' Connor said and Tim's head shot around, his friend's grave tone setting off alarm bells.

'Who?'

'You and Maria.'

'When?'

'Cherry left her phone by the pool, and I was coming to get it when I saw you. Figured it looked pretty intense, so I left you to it.'

Intense? Tim couldn't put it better himself. But how much had his friend witnessed? The kiss or purely the convo…?

'Didn't look like you were talking about the weather, if you get my drift…'

The kiss. *Definitely* the kiss. He cursed.

'Yeah, think I said that too. Is that what has you all…?'

'All what?'

Connor raised his brows. 'Moodier than usual?'

Tim pressed his lips together, his eyes finding Maria through the glass. She was busy making the cocktails in the saloon bar, Trix beside her, chatting away. There was no way they could overhear them. Not even Cherry and Dana could overhear them above the music, but he worried all the same.

'Don't make a thing of it, will you?'

'Why don't you tell me what I'm not making a thing of first and then I can tell you whether I agree. Because I know you, Tim, and you're the last person on earth I would expect to have to talk to about respect and boundaries and what's okay and what's not. She works on my boat and you—'

'It's not like that.'

'No?'

Tim raked a hand through his hair. 'She didn't want me to say anything.'

'This is getting worse by the second.'

'We've met before.'

'Huh? When?'

'She was working in the bar I ended up at after the party last week. Trix was working there too.'

Connor leaned forward, his eyes drifting to Trix and Maria still talking inside. 'Hang on, you mean the bar Trix's uncle owns?'

'Yeah, you know it?'

'I know about it, sure, but it's miles out of the city. Wow, you really did want to get away!'

'That's hardly news.'

'No, but—hang on, so you know *both* of them? And yet none of you said anything when you came on board.'

'I didn't know Trix by name, no. And Maria made it clear she didn't want me to let on.'

'Why?'

'For the same reason you're now getting all preachy with me.'

Connor's brows lifted into his hairline. 'I'm not getting preachy, but there is a line, bro... I take it you two weren't just talking about the weather the night you met either?'

'Connor...' It was a low warning.

'I'm just making sure I have all the facts.'

'The only fact that matters is that she isn't interested. Not any more.'

'Impressed her that much, hey?' he teased, but Tim didn't find anything about this situation funny. 'Quit looking so grouchy. I'm only kidding around, because I'm telling you now, what I saw looked mutual enough to me.'

He'd thought so too, but…

'The words coming out of her mouth suggest otherwise.'

'Did she say why?'

'She says it's the whole crew-guest dynamic, which of course I understand, but…'

'You don't believe her?'

No, he didn't. Worry over her position on the yacht didn't warrant tears. It had been deeper than that. So deep, it had caused her pain. And *that* he wanted to understand. Understand and take away. Because if she hurt, he hurt.

'I don't know. I just know I haven't felt this way since Ellie.'

'*Seriously?*' Connor choked on the dregs of his whisky.

'Don't look so surprised.'

'Seven years, man. Seven years and you meet a random woman in a bar and just like that…'

'I know how it sounds, but I'm telling you, it happened.'

'What happened?'

'That moment, you know, when you just *know*? The lightning bolt.'

'The what now?' He was looking at him like

he'd sprouted three heads, every one of them spouting nonsense. Hell, maybe it *was* nonsense and somewhere along the way he'd lost his grip on reality.

He'd known nothing of her in that moment... nothing other than the fact that she triggered the same intense reaction Ellie once had.

But to feel it again...after all this time.

'Doesn't matter.' He downed the last of his drink with a hiss. 'Forget I said anything.'

'It matters plenty if it's got you thinking about enjoying life again.'

His gaze drifted back to Maria beyond the glass. She had all four drinks on the tray now and Trix was frowning at her, saying something. His neck prickled. Were they talking about him, *them*? Did Trix know? Was she offering her own counsel?

'If you want my advice, just apologise.'

He set his frown on Connor. 'For what, exactly?'

Because Tim knew well enough what he had to apologise for, Connor's take on it however...

'Buggered if I know.' His friend shrugged. 'But it always seems to work for me.'

Tim gave a tight laugh. 'Says the guy who's a self-professed womaniser.'

'Means I have plenty of experience in smoothing things over with the opposite sex, and I'm telling you, one should never underestimate the power of an apology, even when one has done nothing wrong.'

He'd done plenty wrong…pursuing her when she'd said no.

'Hell, maybe you just scared her off with your smile that's so out of practice.'

'Thanks.'

'You gotta admit, it is kinda rusty… But I'm serious, pull her aside and talk to her. Explain how you feel.'

Hadn't he already tried that and look where it had landed him, in even deeper bother with an even bigger reason to apologise. And for that, he did need to get her alone.

'A bit hard when we're always surrounded by people.'

'You want me to talk to her, tell her not to stress about the whole staff—'

'No! I don't want you to talk to her!'

'But it's my boat, I'm effectively her boss, maybe she'd feel more at ease hearing it from me.'

'I can't think of anything worse. And neither could she, I imagine.'

'So, you do it. Most of the crew are down for the night. Russell's up in the wheelhouse on anchor watch. Anya won't venture this way unless something crops up, and I'll distract Trix with some task downstairs.' He pushed up out of his seat. 'Consider the deck yours.'

Maria was on her way back and his racing heart knew it. 'Connor…'

'Come on, ladies,' his friend said, wrapping an arm around each of them. 'Let's take this party below deck… 'Night, Campbell.'

''Night Campbell,' they chorused, folding into Connor's side.

''Night,' he said through gritted teeth.

They passed by Maria, taking their drinks as they went, and leaving her standing there in the middle of the deck, a solitary glass of whisky left on her tray, its colour as rich as her eyes that flickered his way. He gave a small smile, she followed suit, though it stalled when the pumping tunes through the sound system cut to something softer, more sultry, more… *Connor!*

The man himself gave a thumbs-up through the glass, his smile as mischievous as his actions. The man was a goddamn menace.

But then he was gone, a menace no more as he took his women with him, and a dutiful Trix followed. God knew what task he'd assigned his chief stew or for how long she'd be gone, but right now, they were alone.

Just the glittering ocean and the moon and a thrumming beat for a backdrop…and he wasn't just talking about the music.

OhGodohGodohGod…
This was too much.

He was too much.

Too hot. Too broody. Too intense.

His dark shirt adding to the entire vibe as he lounged back on the cream leather sofa, legs spread, eyes watching, waiting...anticipating.

He wants his drink, doofus!

She hurried forward, keeping her gaze fixed on the table as she swapped his empty glass for the fresh one and prepared to leave. 'Can I get you anything else?' she asked, her voice too small, too distant over the pounding beat of her heart.

She needed to get a grip. Do her job and get to bed. And quick. Because hanging about after dark, with him, was a bad, *bad* idea.

'Maria?'

He was just another man, another rich man at that, and she really ought to know better. She wasn't a teenager daring to overreach. She was a grown-ass woman who knew her place in the world and knew well enough the trouble her feelings could get her into.

'Maria?'

'Yes!' She bit her lip on the outburst. Not cool. Not cool at all. 'Sorry, yes?'

'Will you look at me? Please.'

She released her lip and took a breath, exhaling as she lifted her lashes... Oh, God, those *eyes*. They unravelled her from within.

'What is it?'

It came out harsh, rude even, but man, she just

wanted to get back inside and away from him and the danger.

'I owe you an apology. And I don't want to get it wrong this time.'

You what, now...? She was the one that had fled from him. She was the one snapping at him. She was the one who should be...

She frowned, her knees weakening. 'I don't understand.'

'Will you sit with me a second so I can explain?'

Her knees screamed, *Yes, sit!* But her head...

She glanced around at the deserted deck, the deserted saloon, the sea, the dark shadow of Refuge Cove in the distance...

'It's time you clocked off anyway, it's long past midnight.'

And didn't her dog-tired limbs know it, but so long as the guests were still up, she was still on...

'Surely you can quit treating me as a guest now everyone else has gone to bed,' he said, reading her thoughts so clearly.

'*You* haven't.'

'And I don't need you waiting on me, so please, take a seat. I'd make it an order if I thought you'd obey it quicker.'

Now that put a fire up her. 'Don't push it.'

He smiled. 'That's better.'

She gave a huff of a laugh, grateful that it had

somehow broken the moment that had held her in its grasp. 'I'm glad you enjoy getting my back up.'

'I prefer it to you being meek, because the woman I met last week was anything but meek.'

Heat assaulted her cheeks. Why, oh, why did she have to be a blusher?

'That was different then,' she said, slipping the tray onto the table and perching herself on the sofa's edge. 'You were just a customer in a bar.'

'And now I'm a billionaire on a yacht you think I want you to behave any different?'

A billionaire?

Did he just say...? *Oh, sweet heavens*, what the hell was she doing?

And he wasn't bragging either, he was simply stating a fact...and she shouldn't be surprised, not when the yacht they were bobbing around on had to be worth hundreds of millions...but that was Montgomery's wealth.

'Maria?'

She wet her lips, forced her eyes back to his. 'You said you wanted to apologise?'

He gave a slow nod, the intensity of his gaze sending a flame through her veins, and she gripped her hands in her lap. Focused on steadying her breath rather than the way he was making her feel.

'Yes.'

'I can't even begin to imagine why. Unless...'

Oh God, no! 'You haven't told Mr Montgomery about—about us?'

He shifted in his seat. 'That wasn't why I was apologising, no.'

'But you have, haven't you? Ohnonono, what were you *thinking*?' She launched to her feet, glaring down at him. 'I asked you not to.'

'I know and I'm sorry. It wasn't how you're thinking.'

He was lucky she didn't bite his flamin' hand off as he reached for her, trying to calm her but only infuriating her further. How Montgomery must see her now. How utterly humiliating. How easy. Because she *had* been easy. Giving herself to Tim on that very first night, agreeing to one night…

'And how exactly am I thinking?'

'I don't know, some boastful chat between guys…'

Exactly that!

'But it wasn't. He saw us together on deck earlier. Saw enough to know that something had happened.'

'And you just had to confirm it?'

'He wanted to know what was wrong with me.'

'Wrong with you?'

Another slow nod. She was beginning to find the gesture quite maddening.

'Why would he ask that?'

'He seems to think I'm more out of sorts than normal.'

'And you told him that was down to *me*?'

The guy was gonna get her kicked overboard!

And if they dropped her in Refuge Cove she'd be screwed. Hundreds of kilometres away from Melbourne. Would they expect her to find her own way back too? Money she could ill afford to spend. Could she even *get* a taxi from the cove? She had no clue.

'Don't worry, it's very much my problem, not yours.'

She sank back into the sofa. 'How? How can it be your problem when you've just labelled me the issue? Called me out to your closest friend. Do you think he's gonna keep me on board? *Up-setting* you?'

His mouth twitched, his eyes glinting in the low light. 'I didn't label you as any such thing. And he wouldn't dare fire you mid-charter because of how I feel about you.'

And there he went again, bringing up his feelings for her. Feelings she didn't want to listen to because they only triggered her own.

'We went through this today.'

'We did and that's why I want to apologise. Though I find myself having to apologise for a whole lot more now.'

'I suppose that's my fault too.'

He ran a hand over his stubble, the sudden laughter in his eyes surprising and dizzying.

'I don't think it's funny.'

'I'm not laughing.'

'Your eyes are.'

'Can I help it if I find your argumentative nature amusing?'

'*My* argumentative nature?'

His eyes still danced, a smile playing about his lips now as he reached for his whisky, but he didn't take it up. Instead, he turned the glass in his hand while he considered her and she wriggled in her seat, wishing he wasn't within arm's reach. That his hand wasn't distractingly close as he rolled the whisky around, his fingers calling to mind all the things he had skilfully done with them, all the things she wanted him to do still.

She cleared her throat, lifted her chin and her gaze with it. 'Some apology this is turning out to be.'

'You had me distracted. I'll try again, shall I?'

'Please, because then I might be able to say goodnight and get some sleep.'

'That keen to get away from me again?'

Her conscience squirmed while she kept her lips sealed. She knew how she sounded, but her walls were up and she needed them to stay that way.

'Not that I blame you.'

Huh?

'I'm sorry. Sorry for Connor discovering the truth. Sorry for making you uncomfortable. Sorry for the conversation he witnessed, because we never should have been locked in that discussion in the first place. I never should have pressed you for more when you've made your feelings clear, several times over. So, I'm sorry. But answer me one thing…'

'What's that?'

'Is this purely about the here and now, or is there something you're not telling me, because the way you ran from me today—'

'I told you, I'm part of the crew, there's a code of conduct to follow,' she rushed out. 'This job is important to me and I need the money. I get that you might not understand that with your wealth, but—'

'I'd never put your job at risk. Your position on this yacht is solid. I promise you that.'

Her stomach rolled. He was so sure. So blind to the impossible position she was in. Just like Fraser…

'How? How will you do that when the crew start gossiping about me?'

'Do you honestly think people here will judge you, judge us?'

'Of course they will.'

Though Trix had already made it clear she didn't care. And if she didn't, maybe the rest wouldn't. But none of that mattered because really, she was the one running scared. She was the one using the crew as an excuse, so she didn't have to admit the truth. That the only person who cared was her and she was the one losing all fight now as his sincere gaze burned into hers.

'Why do you care so much about what others think?'

'Spoken like a man who has never been the brunt of vicious gossip before.'

'Believe me, at my level, people have plenty of stuff to say, most of which is unfounded and derogatory.'

'Enough money not to care then.'

'If they mean nothing to me, their words mean nothing. It's as simple as that.'

She gave a muted huff. 'Oh, to not care, I'll envy you that.'

'Why? What happened to you, Maria?'

She swallowed, remembering the whispers, the judgemental stares...

'It doesn't matter.'

'It does to me.'

'The point is, it's different for you. No one will dare say anything to you.'

'And if anyone dared say anything to you, they'd have me to answer to.'

It was a growl, a loaded threat that stole her breath and warmed her through. She almost believed it too. Almost. But hadn't Fraser said the same? All those empty promises... He'd only intervened when the whispers had gotten loud enough to reach him, threatening to reach his family, his wife and his daughters, the community at large…

'And what would you do?' Her laugh rang with cynicism. 'Go to Connor and get him to silence them? Get him to give me a nice juicy bonus too? Or pay me yourself to make up for it?'

Because Fraser had. He'd thrown money at her repeatedly, instead of the love she'd craved.

'That's not what I'm saying.'

'No, are you sure about that?'

'I'd make sure you weren't financially impacted.'

'And my reputation?'

'Trix is your friend. She knows we met before we came aboard, that this isn't some…some weird financial arrangement.'

He looked confused and she couldn't blame him. She sounded irrational. She was being irrational, taking out her past on him, and that wasn't fair. He didn't deserve it.

No, what he deserved was the truth. He'd given her his. Opening up to her about his past, wearing his heart on his sleeve when he'd spoken of his wife, his daughter…and when he'd spoken of his desire for her…his want…

She could destroy that though. Obliterate his desire for her with her own truth.

So why wasn't she doing just that?

She'd like to think it was because she was used to keeping it a secret.

But she knew it had more to do with losing his respect than anything else. Which meant she cared what he thought. Cared too much.

'I'm sorry I made you feel that way, Maria.'

'You need to stop apologising.'

'I don't think I've—'

'I'm not the person you think I am.'

His head shot up. 'And what person is that?'

'I don't know, someone who deserves that look in your eye, the attention you're giving me…'

'I think I should be the judge of that, don't you?'

She stared at him, wishing she could just come clean. If ever there was a reason for him to keep his distance, her past was it. And then she wouldn't have to work so hard to avoid him and the danger he represented, because he'd be avoiding her enough for the two of them.

'And if this is where you say *you don't know me* again,' he said, 'I'll tell you the same thing I did earlier. I *want* to get to know you, if you'll let me.'

'No. You don't.'

'Why? What are you so afraid of?'

'Who says I'm afraid?'

'You did—when you ran from me today. People don't cry and run for no reason, they do it because they're scared…so tell me, what were you running from?'

And that was when she realised his hand now covered hers upon the sofa between them, his palm a soothing balm to her soul…a balm she couldn't accept, because she didn't deserve to heal.

'You wouldn't understand.'

'Try me.'

CHAPTER NINE

TIM HADN'T BEEN aware of taking her hand...

Until she pulled away.

Her warmth still clung to his palm, the echo of her touch tingling and taunting as the chill of her rejection washed over him. He curled his fingers into a fist and forced himself back in his seat.

He'd give her space, if that was what it took to get to the truth. What it took to get to know her.

She ran her teeth over her bottom lip, her lashes lifting as her eyes found his again. 'You'll judge me.'

'Do I strike you as a judgemental person?'

'No, you strike me as an honourable one, and any honourable person would judge me.' She took an uneasy breath. 'I've never talked to anybody about my life before I rocked up at Mickey's Bar. Not even Trix, and she's my best friend.'

Her obvious torment twisted through him. 'You can trust me, Maria.'

She wrung her hands in her lap and he ground

his teeth, battling the desire to untangle her fingers and pull her close…

'I promise.'

She swallowed hard and turned away, pushing herself to her feet, but he sensed she wasn't running. Not this time.

She crossed the deck to the rail, and slowly he followed, not wanting to spook her but unable to keep his distance either.

He glanced down at her beside him, her hands gripping the rail until her knuckles flashed white, eyes unseeing on the moonlit water. The breeze tore strands of hair from her bun, whipping them across her face. He could blame it for the sheen in her eyes, but he knew better—those were the same tears he'd witnessed earlier.

Damn it. He never should have pressed. He should've let it go, just as she'd wanted him to.

'It's okay, Maria. You don't need to tell me. You don't owe me. This was never meant to be anything more than one night. It doesn't warrant—'

'No.' She blinked back the tears, her eyes flitting to his. 'I do need to tell you, then you'll know the person I am and you'll know to let this go.'

He didn't believe it for a second, but if it made her feel better to think it then so be it…

'I'm listening.'

She licked her lips. 'You know enough to know that I wanted to escape my childhood… My parents—they didn't make me feel safe and secure like yours did you.' Her voice quivered with emotion. 'And I'm not using their treatment of me as an excuse either, I'm just trying to explain how I ended up choosing the path I did...'

'Okay.'

'They were angry people. All the time. Angry at their lot in life, angry at each other, angry at me. When words weren't enough, the fists joined in...'

Her eyes flicked to his again—had he cursed? Probably.

But *hell*, the thought of it. The thought of her...

'Everyone knew it too,' she said softly, her gaze back on the horizon but lost in the past. 'Our neighbours all talked, and the more they talked, the worse it got. It wasn't like we could move away either, we never had any money and the police never got involved. It was just another domestic case to them, and I wasn't about to rock up at the station and get another kicking for my efforts.'

He clenched his jaw tight, his entire body vibrating with the desire to hunt these people down and hurt them like they had her. These people who should have been protecting her, nurturing her, *loving* her.

'When I was fourteen, Dad lost his job. That's when everything really turned to shit. I quit school and took all the work I could get. Cash-in-hand. For two years, I worked, giving them some but holding a little back, trying to save enough to get the hell out of there. Only...'

He saw the way her throat bobbed, her lashes flickering as fresh tears came.

'My father found the money and totally lost it. He accused me of doing all sorts to get it, accused me of being selfish too. Told me I was just like my mother, and I was no kid of his.'

'The heartless *prick*.' Acid laced his words, filled with vitriol for the man he'd never met but by God, he wanted to make suffer.

'Turns out, he meant it too. He never thought I was his daughter. All those years treating me like I meant nothing suddenly made so much sense.'

'Did your mum not do anything, did she not...?'

She was shaking her head. 'Mum was wasted most of the time and when she was sober she'd look at me like she didn't recognise me, like I'd somehow grown overnight and she had no idea how I'd got there. I used to fantasise about someone knocking on the door one day and telling them there'd been a mistake, that I'd been taken from my real family at birth and they were here to take me home. Now *that* was a story I would have got behind.'

She gave him a weak smile and he couldn't stop himself from reaching out now, easing away a stray strand that had caught on her lip and tucking it behind her ear.

'I'm so sorry you had to live through that.'

'Yeah, well, I didn't have to live through it any more. He threw me out that night, took the money he saw as his due, threw me some change and told me not to come back.'

He cursed again, his head shaking. It was like some god-awful movie playing out in his head, only it had been her life. 'Where did you go?'

'To the diner where I worked every Saturday. The lady who owned it, she was a sweetheart. Her sister worked in a big house out of town and they were looking for a live-in housemaid. The salary was a pittance, but it would put a roof over my head, food on the table... With her vouching for me, I got the job. I really thought I'd landed on my feet. The house was incredible, like nothing I'd ever seen before... And they were the golden couple, extremely good-looking and successful. He was a world-renowned cosmetic surgeon, often away. And she was a committed socialite with three daughters all under ten. Two were often away at boarding school, the other had a nanny. They were always throwing parties at the weekend and having guests to stay, so we were forever busy. It was fun. For a time. And I was so relieved. Independent at sixteen. Living in a mansion. A solid income, and a life that was mine. No more beatings, no more screaming... I was finally happy.'

'What changed?'

She looked away completely, her neat bun a poor substitute for her eyes that she now hid from him.

'One day, my boss came home early from a business trip.'

Tim's heart sank to his feet, dread keeping it there.

'He wasn't in a good way. He'd lost a patient in the operating theatre. An unexpected complication. I was cleaning his suite when he rolled in, whisky in hand, talking about how this wasn't supposed to happen, not in his line of work. That the patient had lied, but it was his reputation on the line.' She took a shuddery breath, her head dropping forward. 'He was so broken. I'd never seen him like that before.' She turned just enough for him to glimpse her profile, the sheen in her eyes, the tension around her mouth. 'And there I was, sixteen and young, but I'd seen enough in my years to know that whisky wasn't the answer. So I took the glass from him, telling him exactly that, and he thought—he assumed...'

She lifted a hand to her lips and a shiver ran down his spine.

'He didn't, please God tell me he didn't.'

'He did,' she whispered against her fingers. 'I was too stunned to respond at first, I just let him kiss me. I'd never been kissed before and I... I liked it. The idea that this man, this charismatic, successful, well respected, intelligent man could want me...want me when he could take his pick of all the girls. Everyone had a thing for him. And his wife, she was stunning. Stuck up and demanding at times, but stunning. It was her that made me stop. Remembering he was married and how wrong it was. Not to mention how flamin' stupid it would be…risking my job and my home. I pressed him away and he apologised, said he had no idea what had come over him. That he wasn't thinking straight.'

'And you believed him?'

'Yes. And I still believe it was true of that night.'

'But there were other nights?' he said quietly, wishing he could stop the whole sorry tale but knowing this was what he'd asked for all the same. Her truth. Because not hearing it didn't suddenly make it go away. Didn't make it untrue.

And if she'd lived it, he wanted to know it. No matter how much it hurt him too.

'It was another month before anything happened again, but by then we'd become friends, or so I thought. He would seek me out when he returned from work, and we'd talk. I told him about my parents. I told him how coming to work for him had saved me from that life, and he told me about all the fascinating people he would meet and the places he would travel to and how one day he'd like to take me too. He told me about his relationship with his wife, how it was all for show, that neither of them were happy but they stayed together for the girls. That as soon as the girls were old enough, they'd go their separate ways, and he'd be free to see whoever he wanted. He'd be free to see me.'

'So, you had an affair?'

'Yes,' she whispered. 'I'm not proud of it, but I believed him. I believed him when he said he loved me and that he wanted to marry me and that he would just as soon as the time was right. Until then we had to keep it a secret. No one could know.'

'I bet they couldn't.' He shook his head. 'How old was he?'

She swallowed. 'Late thirties.'

'And you were *sixteen*?'

'Seventeen when our relationship changed. And yes, I know how it sounds, like he groomed me or something, and it would be so easy for me to say that's what happened, but it wasn't. I knew what I was doing. I wanted him. For the first time in my life, I felt like someone truly saw me, truly wanted me. I fell hard and I fell fast and he was everything. Until I got pregnant. And then it all changed.'

'*Pregnant*? Oh God, he's Fae's father, isn't he?'

'Yes.'

'My God, *Maria*.'

'His reaction wasn't far off yours.' She gave a twisted smile. 'He wanted me to get an abortion. Said it was best for the baby and for me, but really he was just terrified of our affair getting out. It wasn't just his marriage on the line but the affection of his daughters and his standing in the community too.'

'Because he knew he was in the wrong.'

'We both were.'

'No, *he* was, Maria. You were only just of age, far too young…'

'Old enough to get pregnant and to know I wanted to keep it at all costs.'

'How did he react?'

She huffed. 'When he realised I wasn't going to change my mind he shipped me off to the city. Set me up in a flash apartment, got me the best doctors, paid me enough so I didn't want for anything. Told me everything would be okay so long as I kept quiet. He started to control where I went, who I saw, what I did… When Fae was born it was days before he came to us, and even then he barely looked at her. I realised then that he would never love her like he loved his other daughters. I also realised that he was never going to leave his wife. That it was all just empty promises, and we would forever be his dirty little secret.'

He winced as she used the same label he'd accused her of dismissing him as.

'Yeah…that's why I ran this afternoon.'

'I'm so sorry.'

'You weren't to know.'

He wished he had though. Wished to God

he'd known the whole damn lot because it made so much sense now. Her fixation on her place amongst the crew, her protectiveness over Fae, her fear of messing up a life she'd worked so hard to secure for them both...

'If it had just been me back then I would have run then too, started over, but I had Fae to think about. And knowing that he was willing to pay to support us both...he could afford to give her the kind of life I couldn't, not in my wildest dreams. After the childhood I'd had, I was convinced this was what was best for Fae. She wanted for nothing. I showered her in love while he showered us in money. And for fourteen years, I let him keep a roof over our heads, pay for her schooling, even let him worm his way back in on occasion, but those visits became few and far between as Fae got older and started to ask questions of her own, wanting to know where he was, when he was coming back... He didn't like that.'

Tim cursed, the idea unimaginable to him as a father.

'Eventually, I realised he was doing more damage than good. Damaging us both. After Fae got caught up in a nasty encounter at school, I called him, told him what had happened, and instead of coming to her aid, offering his love, his concern, he offered up a relocation, a different school, and I was done. I told him if he didn't want to know his own daughter, we didn't want to know him in return. I told him I was selling up and taking the proceeds from the sale to start a new life, and I didn't want to hear from him again.'

'And he let you go?'

'When I told him I'd go to the press if he didn't, yeah. That was four years ago now.'

'And you haven't heard from him since?'

'No. And to think I once thought myself in love with him.'

'You didn't know any better.'

'I like to tell myself that but...'

'But nothing. That son of a bitch took advantage, and you know it. If Fae came to you now and told you she'd met a man your age, don't tell me you wouldn't be putting the blame firmly on his shoulders.'

Her eyes shimmered, but she didn't deny it.

He cursed. 'You must look at Connor with those girls and think...'

'Cherry and Dana are almost ten years older than I was, it's different.'

'You still thought it though?'

'For a moment, maybe.'

He inhaled softly. 'I'm sorry, Maria.'

'You need to stop apologising...'

'But I *am* sorry. I'm sorry your parents were horrible human beings that didn't deserve you. I'm sorry that your first love—'

'My only love, if you take Fae out of the equation.'

'I'm sorry it was so messed up. And I'm sorry Connor has brought it back, that I've brought it back by making you relive it.'

'The past is the past, but I can't deny what I was. A mistress willing to be kept and controlled by a man.'

'What you did, you did because you thought it was right for Fae.'

'And what a mess I made of that too. Parents are supposed to protect their children from the bad stuff. She was in the centre of it. And she knew it. All her life she knew she was the forgotten child, the unwanted child...' Her voice cracked. 'And I tried to make him see sense. He didn't have to love me or be there for me, but he should have been there for her, he should have loved her like he loved them. Her pain was my doing.'

'No! Her pain was *his* doing. You're not the villain in this piece. He is. Surely you can see that. He was the married man. He was the one bound by vows. He was the one who betrayed his own family to be with you. And then to control you from afar...what man does that?'

'What mother lets him? For fourteen years I let him...'

'You did what you thought was right.'

'I sometimes wondered if he was right, it would have been better, kinder to have...' she swallowed, one solitary tear escaping as she shook her head. 'But then I wouldn't have Fae, and she is everything to me.'

'You can't think like that,' he said softly. 'And you need to stop hating yourself for it all.'

'I don't hate myself.'

'No?' He cupped her cheek, encouraging her to turn and meet his gaze. She blinked up at him, the vulnerability in her caramel eyes teasing at his heart. 'You were the one who told me I wouldn't want to know you when I knew the truth, but listen to me now when I tell you, you are worthy of knowing, Maria.' He stroked his thumb along her cheek. 'And I'm *glad* you told me, so that I can tell you, right here, right now, that I see you and I still like you…'

Her lashes flickered, the smallest smile quivering on her lips as a flush of colour reached into her cheeks. Her eyes warming too. 'You're just being nice.'

He gave a low chuckle. 'Like someone else once said, I don't do anything for nice's sake.' Then his eyes dipped to her lips… 'And I certainly don't do this.'

He bowed his head, slow enough for her to stop him if she wished, and brushed his mouth against hers, savouring her sweet inhalation and the soft parting of her lips.

'But I'll stop. If this isn't what you want, say so now. But don't tell me it's because I shouldn't want you, because I do.'

* * *

She'd never let anyone see the real her.

And yet she'd let him. And he was looking at her like...

Don't be fooled like you were with Fraser.

But he wasn't Fraser—a married man high on the thrill of the forbidden, of control and secrecy. He was a loving widower, a loving father, and now he was caring for her...in ways that she'd never dreamed of experiencing again. Not like this, with her heart laid bare, her past with it.

And the rush of feeling terrified her, but...

'No,' she whispered. 'I don't want you to stop.'

She buried her fingers in his hair, reaching up as he came down, their mouths melding together in scorching-hot harmony. A moan rose through her throat as she took all that he was gifting her. Acceptance. Heat. Passion as much as compassion.

And hadn't she suffered enough, denied herself enough?

Could she not enjoy a little slice of this, but on *her* terms this time?

Not for forever, but for now?

She leaned back, gazing up into his eyes that devoured her where she stood, and curled her toes into the deck. It would be so easy to forget the end and dream of the future when he looked at her like that. She sucked in a breath as unsteady as she felt. Boundaries. They needed boundaries.

'I want this. I do. But my life with Fae...'

'You don't want anything interfering with it.'

'Any*one*.'

He nodded. 'I get that.'

'Can you get on board with it though?'

His eyes danced, his mouth cocking to the side. 'We're very much *on* board, in every possible sense.'

'I'm serious.'

'So am I.'

And then he captured her lips in a kiss that stripped her of all thought and breath and left her in no doubt he wanted this. His hands roved over her body as she slipped her own beneath his shirt...

'We should take this inside,' he rasped, and she nodded, a pinch of reality breaking in. They still needed to be discreet and—

'Thank God!'

They leapt apart, spinning towards the voice as a chair clattered across the deck.

Maria's heart surged into her throat. *'Dana?'*

'Help!' The girl stumbled up to them, wild-eyed, breathless, a robe wrapped haphazardly around her body. 'Please! It's Cherry—she's not breathing right!'

Maria launched forward, Tim right beside her.

'Where is she?' he demanded.

'In our room.'

'Where's Connor?'

'He's there too.'

They shared a look as they raced inside, her heart beating ten to the dozen as they weaved through the saloon and down the stairs. All the way Dana sobbed, rambling that she didn't understand what had happened, what was wrong, why she'd collapsed...

Collapsed?

Oh, God!

The moment they stepped into the cabin, a chill washed over her. Montgomery stood with his back against the wall, half naked, deathly pale, his terrified gaze locked on the girl sprawled across the bed, limbs slack, skin ghostly pale.

Tim cursed. 'What the hell happened?'

Maria raced forward, dropping to her knees beside Cherry. The girl's lips were blue, her chest barely moving. She checked her pulse. Faint but there, far too slow.

'Did she take anything?' Maria glanced up at a frozen Montgomery, then Dana.

'I... I don't know!' Dana stammered out.

Maria eased Cherry's head back, checked her airway. Still clear, thank God.

'I don't think so. We were just drinking. Everything was fine and then—and then she zoned out.'

'Connor?' Tim gripped his friend by the shoulders, forcing his attention on him. 'Did she take anything?'

But Montgomery remained mute.

'I'm pretty sure she's overdosing,' Maria said, shifting Cherry's body into the recovery position. 'It could be alcohol, but her lips…'

Tim broke away from Montgomery, checking every surface; he pushed open the bathroom door—'Got it!'

He came out of the bathroom with a small compact, dusted with the remnants of something, and a tiny packet of pills. Maria rushed up and took the packet. Blasted opioids!

Dana shook her head frantically. 'I didn't… I don't…'

'What's going on?' Trix came flying into the room, PJs on, toothbrush in hand. She spluttered out a curse full of toothpaste.

'Trix!' Maria blurted. 'Do you know if there's naloxone on board?'

Her friend shook her head, swallowed. 'I doubt it.'

'Connor?' Tim strode up to him, gave him a shake. 'Answer her. Naloxone?'

'I don't even know what that is.' Montgomery shook his head, swallowed. His bare chest heaving with the motion and exaggerating the scars he bore down one side. Scars she hadn't seen before today. 'There shouldn't be any drugs on board. You know I don't—'

'Trix, get Russell to issue a mayday,' Maria demanded, hurrying back to Cherry's side. 'She needs airlifting. Now!'

Trix nodded and ran.

Dana let out a choked sob. 'Is she going to die?'

'Not if I can help it,' Maria said, unwilling to give false promises.

Damn drugs and the fools who thought they would never fall foul of them.

'I should've noticed. I should've—' Dana's knees buckled, and Tim caught her before she hit the floor. Guiding her to a chair, he looked back at Maria. 'What can I do?'

'Just keep an eye on Dana,' she said, then she glanced at Connor, who was stumbling forward, his eyes fixed on Cherry.

'I don't allow drugs on board. If I'd known...' He dragged a hand down his harrowed face, looking every one of his forty plus years now.

'I've got her,' Maria said, trying to reassure him, but she wasn't convinced he heard her. He was living in his own hell. She looked to Tim for help.

'Connor, it's not your fault,' he said. 'Go get some air, yeah?'

'I can't just leave her.'

'You'd be better getting dressed and greeting the rescue crew.'

With a last long look at Cherry, he staggered out.

'You knew exactly what to do,' Tim said into the sudden quiet.

'Mickey trains up all his staff...' And this

wasn't Maria's first overdose encounter. Likely wouldn't be her last either. She blew out a breath. 'We're not out of the woods yet.'

'No.' He gave her a small, firm nod. 'But you just gave her a damn good chance.'

'Let's hope so.' Maria glanced down at the fragile blonde and prayed he was right.

Some evening. From dinner to impromptu therapy to a truly explosive kiss and now this… Her stomach was in knots, her hastily snatched dinner threatening to return.

She took the girl's hand and checked her pulse again.

'Come on, Cherry, you're a fighter. Fight this.'

CHAPTER TEN

As THE RESCUE helicopter lifted off, its blades slicing through the night air, Tim stood rooted to the foredeck. A tightness coiled in his chest—not just from the gravity of the moment, but from the woman beside him. The woman who had kept her head while everyone else was losing theirs. The woman who'd spent most of her life surrounded by people who should have loved her and cared for her and done nothing of the sort.

Aside from Fae, of course. The most important person in her world, who was lucky enough to be loved and protected by the best. Her mum.

But who was there to protect her...?

She had Trix, sure. And Bob across the hall. Mickey too. And he knew from his talks with the landlord that he was trying to do his best by his tenants. Even if that desire had led him down a path of poor decision-making. Something Tim could help with. Something he *was* helping with. But it wasn't enough.

Tim wanted to be there for her, and that driving need was as instinctive as all the other feelings she'd dusted off within him.

'You okay?' he asked as the flashing red lights of the helicopter disappeared over the headland.

'Yeah,' she said softly. 'I just hope Cherry will be.'

'She's stable,' he said, fighting the urge to take her hand in his. 'That's something.'

'And it's all thanks to you, Maria,' Connor said from the other side of him—more composed now, but no less shaken. 'I mean it. You were incredible. If you hadn't taken charge like you did...'

'I did what anyone else would've done given the chance.'

Tim took in the set of her shoulders, the quiet strength in her stance despite the exhaustion lining her face, and admiration swelled within him. For *everything* she had done, not just tonight, but before then too. Breaking away and starting afresh. Twice over.

'I didn't do it,' Connor said.

'You were in shock,' she replied gently.

'Maria's right,' Tim said, placing a placating hand on his friend's shoulder. 'Don't be so hard on yourself.'

But Connor wouldn't be told. He radiated tension. Tension and guilt. And Maria could see it too, her concerned gaze flitting between them both.

'I'll just...' she gestured to where Trix had Dana wrapped in a blanket off to the side, the girl's hushed sobs only just audible now '…go and see if I'm needed.'

He nodded.

'Tell Dana our ride will be here in a few hours,' Connor said. 'If you and Trix can make sure all their things are packed up and good to come with us.'

'No problem.'

She looked back at Tim, some unspoken message in her gaze, and he gave her the smallest of smiles, his eyes following as she walked away.

'You're right about her,' Connor murmured. 'She is pretty special.'

The coil within his chest turned that bit further. 'She is.'

They watched in silence as Maria embraced Dana and Trix, the women all offering one another support.

'Did you manage to talk earlier?' Connor asked. 'Before everything…'

He gave a slow nod. 'Yeah, we talked.'

'And?'

And things had been better, but now…

'We cleared the air.'

'Good. That's good.'

Was it? She'd been happy to indulge in whatever this was so long as it didn't impact on her life with Fae—it was better than nothing, but was it enough?

Tim had never thought himself a greedy man, but when it came to Maria...

And now their trip had come to such a cataclysmic end, reality beckoned, her sacred life with Fae...

'Take *Celeste* on, won't you?'

'What?' Tim tugged his gaze from the women now heading inside to frown at Connor. 'How do you mean?'

'*I mean*, don't quit the trip because I'm leaving with Dana.'

'But Connor, it's your yacht...'

'So? The crew are all booked in, Rio flew in from the States to cater for this, and hell, Trix and Maria deserve some downtime after what I've put them through this evening.'

'You didn't put them through anything, you had no idea the drugs were on board.'

He gave a soft huff. 'I should have seen the signs.'

'We *all* should have seen the signs if that's how you're going to look at it.'

'But I froze down there. All I saw was...' he swallowed, his skin turning ashen as he pocketed his fists '...all I saw was them. Lifeless and...'

He gripped Connor's shoulder, felt the tremors rolling through his friend's body. 'Hey, it's okay.'

'It's not okay. I felt as helpless as I did then, only this time I should have been able to do something.'

'Rather than beat yourself up over something you could have no control over, why not see it as a sign?'

His brow creased up, his bloodshot eyes zoning in on Tim's. 'A sign?'

'Like maybe it's time to ease back on the partying, find some real meaning to life again?'

'Says the guy who's simply been existing for the last seven years.'

'Don't worry, I've had my wakeup call too.'

His brows lifted. 'You mean Maria?'

'Yeah, I mean Maria.'

Connor almost smiled, his shoulders relaxing as he eased round to face him fully. 'Which means you have to continue on without me, spend some time with her, see whether this could be something more...'

'And what about you?'

'I'll get Dana to the hospital, see Cherry back on her feet and then we'll see.'

'Mr Montgomery?' Captain Kali joined them. 'What would you like us to do, sir?'

Connor looked at Tim. 'What do you say?'

What could he say when he finally felt like he was living again?

'If you're sure.'

Now Connor smiled. 'Good man.' He turned to Kali. 'You're going to continue on to Gabo Island, Captain, just as soon as Dana and I leave.'

'Very well, sir.'

'I know I don't need to say it, but take good care of my friend here, see he gets everything he needs. But I also want you all to get some downtime in. Treat it as something of a pleasure cruise. You deserve it after tonight.'

'That's very kind of you, sir.'

Connor gave Kali a brusque nod, guilt still tugging at the edges of his smile. 'Assure everyone that their salary plus bonus will be paid in full for the charter.'

'Will do.'

Kali walked away and Connor raked an unsteady hand through his hair. 'If one good thing can come of tonight, it's seeing you make some changes for the better.'

'Right back at you.'

'If there's anything more I can do to thank you, to thank Maria too, you only have to say the word.'

'Actually…' Tim checked the master stateroom beyond the glass, the women were no longer in their eyeline, but Maria was still on his mind as ever. 'You don't happen to know a decent private investigator, do you?'

Connor cocked his head. 'Are we talking corporate or private?'

'Private. Very much private.'

'Can I ask why?'

'You can ask…'

His eyes probed, looking for the answer Tim wasn't prepared to give.

'Is everything okay? With you? Sasha?'

'Yeah, everything's fine, just asking for a friend.'

'Heard that one before.' He pulled out his phone and worked the screen. 'If it's personal, you'll want this one. She's good. Real good.'

Tim's phone buzzed in his pocket. 'Thanks.'

'No.' He pulled him into a hug. 'Thank you.'

Hours later, with the departure of Montgomery and Dana, and a skeleton crew manning the yacht, Maria and Trix had retired to their cabin to get some sleep before they set sail for Gabo Island.

But Maria couldn't sleep.

Her mind wouldn't stop taunting her with Cherry's lifeless body. How close she had come to losing her fight and the idea that somewhere in the world Cherry's mother would have been none the wiser. Helpless to save her.

Didn't matter that Maria knew Fae's stance on drugs mirrored her own, the fragility of life and that of your child's was a burden every good parent carried, and the night's events with Cherry had thrust that constant weight to the fore.

She wanted to call Fae just to hear her voice, but to call now would only give Fae cause to worry and that would entirely defeat the point of calling.

Trix gave a loud snore and turned over on the

bunk beneath her. Her friend clearly wasn't struggling in the sleep department. But then she wasn't also battling the knowledge that not too far away Tim would be lying in his giant cloud of a bed alone…alone when she could be…no, don't go there.

Because heaven knew where they stood now. After all she had told him and the kiss they had shared…then the near tragedy…was it any wonder she was still abuzz with adrenaline and worry and going out of her mind?

Biting back a groan, she threw off her sheets. Maybe a dose of fresh air would cleanse her of the lot.

Unlikely, but it had to be better than this.

She slipped from the room and into the quiet hallway. After the chaos of the night, the deserted stairs and hallways were eerily silent, the low glow of the courtesy lights and the gentle creak and roll of the ship adding to the freakish vibe. That was until she broke out onto the swim deck and then the entire world opened up in breathtaking fashion.

With the moonlit ocean on her left, stretching for as far as the eye could see, and the dark shape of the headland with its secluded, crescent-shaped cove to her right, it was quite possibly the most beautiful sight she had ever seen. The mystical glow to the bright white sand against the granite rocks and the shadowy backdrop of eucalyptus trees that reached up into the star-studded sky above…it didn't look real.

She took a breath and another, the tension in her shoulders easing…

'Couldn't sleep?'

She gasped, her body jolting as she clutched a hand to her chest and spun to find Tim leaning against the wall of the yacht. His relaxed stance telling her he'd been there long before she had.

'Sorry, I didn't mean to startle you.'

She licked her lips. She'd been wrong before… *he* was the most beautiful thing she had ever seen. His hair in sexy disarray, his eyes so dark they were almost black, the moon highlighting every chiselled feature—his cheekbones, strong jaw, bare chest, each undulating ridge to his abs— before her gaze reached his black shorts and snapped back up again.

'I thought you were in bed.'

'I couldn't sleep either.'

He pushed out of the shadows and came towards her, his gaze raking over her. From her simple vest to her tiny shorts to her bare feet, she felt every exposed inch of skin as it tingled against the sea breeze. The tingles multiplying as his eyes swept back up, resting an extra beat on her breasts where she knew her body betrayed every salacious thought.

'Are you okay?' she whispered

'Yeah, you?'

'Yeah.'

His eyes narrowed on hers. 'Why don't I believe you?'

'Perhaps because you're lying as much as I am.'

'Do you want a hug?'

Her breath caught. Did she want a *hug*? She wanted so much more than a *hug*. But there was something about the question, the offer...

When had a man asked her that? Asked with such care and concern and...*oh, my God...* Wordlessly, she stepped forward and he opened up his arms, wrapping them around her as she leaned into him.

She breathed in his warmth, his scent, his solidity and everything about her pulsed and settled. She listened to the waves rolling and his heart beating and took all the comfort he was offering.

'Are you cold?' he murmured, his breath disturbing the hair on her head.

'No.'

How could she possibly be cold with his welcome heat pressing into her?

'You're shivering.'

'I think it's just the adrenaline wearing off.'

And the shock of her reaction to him.

He gave a low hum, the vibration working its way through his body and into her own.

'Connor was right, you were incredible tonight. The way you held your cool and knew just what to do.'

'I told you, Mickey makes sure we're trained up. It doesn't matter how hard he works to keep the drugs out, they always find their way in. And it's better to be prepared than in denial about it.'

Another low hum.

'You weren't too bad yourself, you know.' She lifted her head to meet his gaze. 'You saved Dana from hitting the floor, gave her a shoulder to cry on. You were there for your friend, too.'

And he was here for her now…

His mouth tugged to one side, dark eyes burning into hers. 'Glad I'm good for something.'

'You're good for a whole lot more,' she said softly.

'Are you flirting with me?' It was a low growl, the sound teasing against her chest. 'Careful, Maria, because my restraint is hanging by a thread.'

She nipped her lip. Flirting? Not intentionally, no. She'd been serious. She'd never wanted to lean on a man, depend on a man, to the extent that she did him in this moment. And that was bad. Bad. Bad. Bad!

But the chemistry…

'You know what I want?' she breathed.

His hooded gaze fell to her lips.

'I have a fair idea, but why don't you tell me?'

'To take a stroll.'

'A *stroll?*' His eyes sparkled, his mouth twitching with laughter. He didn't believe her, not for a second. And she couldn't blame him. She didn't believe her either.

'I want to be on that beach, feeling the sand between my toes as I watch the sun rise.'

She turned in his hold, leaned back against him as she took in the moonlit cove and tried to press mute on the crazy flutterings inside. All the wants and the dreams that were trying to rise up under the power of his gaze.

It was just shock and the comedown from the night's events messing with her mind. Making her want for more. Dream for more. With a man so far out of her reach he might as well be on the moon up there...

'Then let's go.'

'What?' She turned her head to meet his eye.

'Let's go to the beach.'

'*Now?*'

'Sure, why not?'

'Because we're due to set sail soon.'

'Who says?'

'Captain Kali.'

'Only because she's following Connor's last instruction to continue the trip as planned.'

'Exactly.'

'But we're the masters of this voyage now—you, me, the entire crew—and if we want to set sail a little later, who's to say no?'

She chewed the corner of her mouth and he turned her back to face him.

'Do you honestly think...' he said, stroking the hair back from her face in that way she was coming to savour '…anyone would take issue with leaving a little later?'

She thought of Trix still sleeping and of the deckhands who'd been brought in to assist during the night when they should've been catching up on their Z's. They could all do with the lie-in.

'Will you clear it with Captain Kali first?'

'I'll go one better and get the RIB too.'

'We don't need the RIB, I can swim it.'

'Okay, Miss Olympic Swimmer Wannabe, I believe you, but we're taking the RIB.'

'Do you know how to handle a RIB?'

He stared back at her, unimpressed by the suggestion that he couldn't, and she smiled. 'Okay, let me just change.'

She started to move off and he tugged her back. Surprise had her rolling right into his chest as his mouth claimed hers. *Oh, my!* The flutters fused into a fire, spreading through her abdomen as her knees turned to jelly, and she clung to his shoulders for dear life.

'Now,' he murmured against her lips, 'you can go.'

She blinked up at him in wonder…wonder and fear. And not just of falling literally, falling metaphorically too. Because it wasn't just her knees that had gone all soft, her heart was racing that way too.

And that wasn't okay.

That wasn't okay at all…

CHAPTER ELEVEN

TIM WATCHED HER GO, his heart lighter for seeing her smile again.

Lighter still to see the playful spark in her gaze. He hadn't felt this attuned to another in so long, his mood so easily swayed by theirs. Somewhere his head was telling him to exercise caution, but his heart beat louder.

And that was what he was listening to twenty minutes later as he helped her onto the RIB. The first fingers of dawn reached into the bay, subtle hues of rose and amber stretching from the sky to the rugged green hills and glass-like sea. The air carried with it the scent of salt and eucalyptus and promised another beautiful day in paradise.

'Wow,' she exclaimed beside him, her face lit with it all as he sped towards the beach. Her hair and thin white shirt billowing back as her caramel eyes shone with the rising sun.

'Wow indeed.'

Her eyes flitted to him, her smile soft. She knew exactly to what—to whom—he was referring, and he didn't care. Not any more. He'd been so scared of sharing his heart with another for so long, that now he was open to the possibility he couldn't hold back if he tried.

'It's hard to believe that life can be so cruel when there is such beauty in the world.'

'I know what you mean,' he said, slowing the boat as they approached the shore and bringing it to a gentle stop in the sand.

'Okay, I eat my words,' she said as he hopped off to drag it further up the beach. 'You can definitely handle a RIB.'

'My parents were big on sailing. Most holidays as a kid were spent on the water.'

'That sounds amazing.'

'It was.'

He reached up to help her down and she came willingly, her hands soft on his shoulders, her eyes smiling into his…but there was a hesitation there. An uncertainty. Was she nervous to be alone with him here? Surely not—not after everything they'd shared, but then, maybe that *was* the problem… the weight of it. The intensity.

He slipped his hands around her waist, her warmth teasing at his palms as he swung her to the ground. He held her steady as she settled, her eyes still hooked in his, hands still soft on his shoulders. He caressed the exposed skin just above the waistband of her shorts, felt the tremor within her. Was that a trapped whimper too?

'So how does it feel?'

She released her lip, the flesh all plump and glossy and tugging at his gaze.

'Feel?' she whispered.

'To be on the sand.'

She looked down at her feet, wriggled her toes and gave a sweet little sigh. 'Like heaven.'

Her eyes returned to his, their golden depths more alluring than the sunrise.

God, he wanted to kiss her. Kiss her and not stop.

And she wanted a stroll, not to be ravished.

'We best move before I do the other thing on my mind.'

She gave a soft laugh as he pulled away, taking his offered hand and letting him lead her along the deserted shoreline. For a while, the only sounds were the morning chorus of the birds and the gentle lapping of the waves. Then she slowed and looked up at him.

'Thank you for this.'

'I didn't really do anything.'

'You made it happen.'

'I'm just glad you came.'

'Me too. It's been a long time since I've done something like this...'

'What? Watched the sunrise? Enjoyed a walk on the beach?'

'Both.'

'But you live so close to the sea...'

'Not close enough when you always have something more important to be doing. Working. Cleaning. Mum duties…'

'You and Fae don't go together?' he said, pausing to frown down at her.

'I think she's a little old for building sandcastles on the beach these days, don't you?' She was trying to brush it off, but he couldn't miss the underlying sadness in her voice. The way she released his hand and continued on without him…

'What do you do for fun together?'

'Watch movies, eat rubbish. I'll cook her favourite meals, and she'll eat enough for two.' She threw him a smile, but it didn't reach her eyes. 'We'll take a walk along Merri Creek when we get a decent bit of time off together.'

'And holidays?'

She looked away but he'd already seen the reply she wouldn't give—what holidays?

He swallowed his curse and focused on the moment they were in, taking her hand once more as they walked.

'Do you know why it's called Refuge Cove?' she asked.

Was she trying to change the topic? Probably. And he was willing to roll with it, but inside…inside, he was desperate to change her reality. And he knew he was interfering enough by addressing her living issues with Mickey. Something he couldn't bring himself to tell her because he knew her pride wouldn't stand for it.

But what about the rest? All those long hours working, the lack of time for her and Fae, none of that would change…

'I didn't think it warranted that level of thought,' she teased, and he forced a smile.

'You probably know how treacherous the Bass Strait can be…'

The look on her face suggested otherwise.

'It's considered one of the roughest seas in the world.'

'I'm regretting asking now…'

'Don't worry, the conditions are good, but if things change there are places like these along the way where we can seek shelter. Hence its name. Sailors have been using this cove to hide from the elements for years. And you can't deny, it looks appealing too.'

'Especially at this time of day…' she said, walking up the sandy bank at the edge of the cove and taking a seat so that she could look out over it all.

'Can we sit here a little?'

'Sure.'

He settled back against the boulder beside her and she surprised him by leaning into him, her blissful sigh music to his ears.

'It's so very beautiful.'

He kissed her hair on impulse. 'It is.'

'Too perfect to be true.'

'And yet, it is true.'

'Is it though?' she murmured, and he had to wonder, did she mean the view or *this,* the rising connection between them?

'I can pinch you, if you like…'

'I'm serious. Doing things like this, enjoying things like this…it might be normal for you, but for me it's the stuff of dreams.'

'I *used* to do stuff like this, but it's been a long time for me too.'

Her eyes were full of scepticism as they met his.

'I mean it, Maria. You've got me living my life again. Seeking out the joy in it. And for that, I'm grateful.'

But what about after? When—if—they parted ways, what would his life be then?

'If I had the money you did, I'd be making every holiday about seeing the world,' she said, folding back into his side. 'Taking time to properly see it and enjoy it.'

There came his wealth again…

'I wasn't always this wealthy, you know. My father was a builder and my mother an architect. My childhood was spent in your average street, at a mainstream school, no bells and whistles. Their hard work really paid off when I hit my teens, but that came with its own downside too.'

'Like?'

'Like being sent away to school. I wasn't lying

when I told you I wanted to run back home. I missed them. But eventually I found my feet, my friends, Connor. And I knew my parents were only doing it because they wanted me to have the best education, and they knew they weren't around enough. But they always made up for it in the holidays. Taking extended leave from the business to travel and spend time with me.'

'You don't have any brothers or sisters?'

'No. I think they would have liked to, but it just never happened for them. It's probably another reason Connor and I are so close.'

'Where do they live now?'

'They have a small farm in the Blue Mountains. Mum loves her horses just as much as Dad loves his boats, and they split their time between there and their travels. Right now, they're cruising along the Danube River.'

'Still big sailors then…'

'Seeing the world one cruise at a time, though now they prefer someone else to be at the helm while they do it. More time for them to enjoy one another and see the sights.'

She smiled as she swept her windswept hair out of her face. 'Still very much in love too?'

'Oh, yes.'

Her smile turned wistful. 'Must be nice. To have that in your life all these years. No wonder you're so…'

His ears pricked, his heart too…

'So?'

She nipped her lip. 'Nothing.'

'You can't just say that and then…'

'You're not your typical billionaire.'

'Know a lot of billionaires, do you?'

She gave a husky laugh. 'Fair point. You just surprise me, that's all. You're…softer.'

'S-softer?' he choked out.

'Don't get me wrong, you're all chiselled too.' Her cheeks warmed. 'But the way you talk about your family, your daughter, your…' she swallowed, her voice hushed '…wife.'

'Billionaires are capable of loving just as much as the next man.'

'I know. I guess I just… I would expect you to mask it more.'

'I tried that once. Ellie would have none of it.'

She gave a tender chuckle. 'I think I would have liked her.'

'Everyone liked her. She had a heart big enough for the both of us and she insisted on showing it every day. After she died…' He watched the froth on the waves form and dissipate, felt his pain ebb and flow with it and realised Connor was right. Talking about Ellie made him feel better, not worse. Especially when Maria was so willing to listen. 'I guess I shut down again. People would ask how I was, probe and probe, and it would only make me clam up more. Then I met you and suddenly, it's all coming out again.'

'Why do you think that is?'

'I don't know.' He considered it. 'Maybe it's guilt.'

She stiffened. 'Guilt?'

'For meeting someone who made me feel like she once had.'

He sensed the way his words pulsed through her. But, good or bad, he couldn't take them back. And he didn't want to.

'Like it's some sort of betrayal. But by talking about her to you, it actually feels the opposite. Like I'm sharing the part of me that will always belong to her, with you.' He shook his head. 'Sorry, I'm making no sense.'

She pulled his arm around her front, cuddling in deeper. 'No, you're making perfect sense. I'm glad you told me about her.'

'I am too,' he whispered, realising just how true it was. 'Talking to you has made me realise I was doing her a disservice by not talking about her. Not letting people around me talk about her too. Not sharing those moments with Sasha. You've helped me realise that I can focus on the joy we shared for all the years we were together, rather than get caught up in the pain of the end.'

She looked up at him, her eyes glistening. 'I'm glad I've been able to give you that.'

'Me too.' He stroked her cheek, lost himself in her eyes that were so very different to Ellie's but no less evocative. 'You're special, Maria. And I wish someone had shown you the value of true love before now. Like Ellie showed me.'

She licked her lips. 'I think that might be one of the sweetest things anyone has ever said to me.'

And then she kissed him. Her hands lifting into his hair as she turned to him fully and he eased back into the sand, taking her with him. Glorifying in her kiss and the press of her body as she settled over him.

'Thank you,' she murmured, her palm resting against his cheek as she met his gaze.

'What for?'

'For making me *feel* special.'

His heart pulsed, his chest tightening around it. *God*, this woman. She owned him. His every thought, every feeling. And instead of running scared like his head told him to, he was surrendering to it. Because he knew the power of it, the rarity and its worth.

And yes, it had the potential to cripple him anew.

But he realised something else as he gazed into her eyes. He realised if he had his time over with Ellie, he wouldn't take a different path. He wouldn't choose not to know her, not to love her, because of the pain that came after.

And he wasn't willing to take a different path now. Though choosing the path for himself was one thing, encouraging Maria to join him on it…

'*This* is special, Maria. What we have. It doesn't come along often but when it does…'

'We need to make the most of it.'

'Yes. And I don't just mean now, I mean tomorrow and the day after and the day after that…'

She pressed a finger to his lips. 'Let's not talk about the future. If tonight has taught me anything, it's that life's too short to spend it dwelling on what might be. Can we just…live in the moment and enjoy it?'

He kissed her finger away. 'Sure.' Though he wanted to press for precisely that—a future. 'If enjoying it means more of that kiss right now.'

She swept her thumb over his bottom lip, her eyes tracing the move. 'Do you think we're alone enough?'

'There's no one around but the birds.'

'And the bees?' Her laughter caught in her throat as he slipped his hand beneath her shirt.

'Those too.'

He savoured her whimper as he caressed her skin, cupping her breast in his palm and teasing its tautened peak over the top of her bikini.

'Tim…' she moaned, arching into his touch.

'Is that a request for more?' he murmured, rolling her under him and deepening their kiss. Desperate to drive her to the brink, right here, on the beach.

He eased back to gaze down at her, marvelling

at her beauty as he slowly unbuttoned her shirt. 'Because I'm all for giving you more.'

Her eyes gleamed up at him, silently pleading—dark, hungry, full of need.

He swept the shirt away from her skin, his own need rising with the sight of her, all flushed and eager, her breasts shifting with every shortened breath she took.

'We don't have any protection,' she whispered, and he smiled.

'We don't need any protection for what I have in mind...'

Her mouth fell into a delectable but silent O.

'Do you want me to stop?'

She lifted her hands into his hair. 'Absolutely not.'

And so he didn't, not until she was crying out his name and he felt sure, so sure, she wanted it all too.

The now, the next, the future.

All with him.

'Well, hello there...' Trix gave her a flirty wave from her reclined position on a sunbed beside the upper deck pool, her bikini as bright and as yellow as the umbrella-adorned drink in her hand.

'Is that...'

'A piña colada done Trixy-stylee?' She eyed her over her sunglasses as she toyed with the straw. 'Why, yes, yes, it is. You want one?'

'Trix, it's not even noon!'

'Hey, don't you be judging me, rolling home after sun-up.' She gave a giggle. 'Or should that be sailing home? Maybe a Sex on the Beach is more your style...'

'Trix!'

'Where's your Adonis anyhow?'

'He's not my Adonis, and *shh*,' she said, scanning the entire area for an unsuspecting eavesdropper. 'Someone will hear you.'

'You think everyone doesn't know? You'd have to be blind not to see the sparks coming off you both.'

'Oh, God!' Maria's cheeks burned as her stomach squirmed, not again.

'Hey, don't worry about it, no one here cares. We're all on holiday now remember, orders from the boss.'

'Still...' Maria dropped down onto the sunbed beside her, snatched Trix's drink from her hand and took a long drag on the straw.

'Hey, take it easy,' Trix said, shoving her glasses into her hair and sitting up to face her. 'It really is okay. Everyone's on cloud nine to be getting a hefty paycheck and a surprise break. It's fun all the way, darl, enjoy it.'

Fun. That was what it was. Fun.

A fling. Not a relationship that could end in disaster.

So why did it feel like her heart was hurtling headlong into precisely that?

She swallowed the nervous bubble, gave a smile. 'You're right.'

'That's my girl!' Trix tapped her knee and retrieved her drink, settling back into the sunbed as she took a sip. 'So where is he? Don't tell me you exhausted him and he's now taking a nap to recover?'

'I swear you have a one-track mind!'

'It's my mind, my problem.'

Maria shook her head with a laugh. 'He had a work call to make.'

'Working? On a day like this…sucks to be a badass billionaire, I guess.'

'Don't you think it's weird though?'

'What?'

'*Us not* working?'

'Weird, yeah, but in the best possible way. So I take it I've lost my roomie?'

'Your roomie?'

'You've seen the bathtub in that stateroom, right? With all those massage jets…' She wagged her eyebrows. 'You need to get yourself moved in.'

'We have two nights left, Trix.'

'All the more reason to get packing, don't you think?'

Maria didn't know what to think because her

body was too busy overriding her head at every opportunity.

'Ohnononononono.' Trix shot back up. 'Honey, please tell me you're not getting in deep with this guy?'

'W—*what*?' she choked out. 'Why on earth would you say that?'

'Because you look like you're overthinking it, and if you're overthinking it, you're making it into more than it is.'

'Of course I'm not.'

'F is for fun, honey, it's also for fling, and a fling doesn't warrant all this thought and feeling…well, save for the orgasmic kind, of course.'

'I know what a fling is, Trix.'

'So why are you stressing?'

Why was she stressing?

Maybe because she'd got the distinct impression that Tim was starting to reach for more… That when he'd told her of his feelings, of how special their connection was, there was a part of her that had reached for it too.

And that was why she'd cut the conversation dead. Telling him not to talk of the future. Telling him to make it about the now. Because everything was safe in the now. Fae was at home, blissfully unaware of their fling, and their fling was as finite as the charter.

In a few days she would return home and life would go back to being as it had been. As it should be. In the meantime, she had a gorgeous man and a superyacht at her disposal…

'You know what, Trix?' She got to her feet and smacked her thighs. 'I've changed my mind, a Sex on the Beach it is.'

'Attagirl! And while you're at it, remind that badass billionaire of yours he's supposed to be on holiday too. Montgomery's orders.'

CHAPTER TWELVE

A SUDDEN RAP on his door had Tim's head snapping up. 'Yes?'

Maria burst in, a pineapple-topped cocktail in hand and the biggest smile on her face. 'Quick, quick! You have to come! There are whales!'

She grabbed his hand and tugged, her excitement making him laugh as he closed the lid on the surveyor's report and let her lead him out. He didn't want to tell her he'd seen whales before. Whales, dolphins, seals...the whole gamut. Swam with them, too. Her joy was too infectious.

As was the sight of her hurrying into his room like she belonged there. Whether it was the morning they'd shared, the cocktails or the downtime, he was just glad to see it.

'Look!' She pointed as they broke out onto the aft deck, her eyes sparkling and wholly captivating. 'Have you ever seen anything so amazing?'

Every moment with her, *yes*.

'Your first sighting?' he asked, dragging his gaze from her to watch as the knobbly head of a humpback broke through the deep blue surface several metres away, a small calf following a heartbeat later, its tail flipping up as it swam in perfect sync beside its mother.

She nodded, inhaling softly. 'It's so sweet how they stick so close together.'

'They'll stay like that for about a year,' he murmured.

'While she nurses it?'

'Nurses it, protects it, helps it to swim…she's effectively using her slipstream to tow them along—taking on more work so they don't have to.'

She gave a small laugh. 'A mother after my own heart.'

Another whale surfaced a little further out, sending a spray of mist into the air, and she gasped, her eyes widening. 'Do you think that's dad?'

'Unlikely, they're not known for sticking around. But I reckon he's their escort now.'

'*Escort?*'

'That's what they call the protector in the pod— the bull that keeps predators and other males at bay…'

'Wow, is it normal to be jealous of whales?'

His heart protested, beating against his ribcage. He knew she was teasing, but still…

'I wouldn't be too jealous. He's only hanging around to get one thing.'

Her eyes flicked to his. 'Oh!'

'Yes, oh.' He grinned. 'Sometimes another cow takes on the protective role but, judging by his slightly smaller size, I'd say he's a bull. They normally hang around in the background unless they see a reason to make themselves known.'

'You think they see the yacht as a threat?'

'Possibly.'

'You seem to know a lot about them—is this from your parents and all your holidays on the water?'

'Them. And Ellie.'

Her hand pulsed around his as she turned to look up at him, her smile as bittersweet as his own. 'Yeah?'

'She loved all marine life. We'd go diving several times a year. Different places, different things to see. She had her bucket list too.'

'Another mother after my own heart. I hope you managed to tick off plenty…' she said, her voice thick with the unsaid—*in the short time you had.*

'We did.'

And the desire to do the same for Maria—*with Maria*—pulled at him. Incessant. Unrelenting. There was so much she hadn't seen…

'If you love this,' he said, a plan forming, 'you're going to love Gabo Island.'

'You've been before?'

'My parents used to take me as a kid and then

I took Ellie—it was one of her favourite places, Sasha's too...'

'Tell me about—'

She broke off, her eyes flicking to the right of him as Anya appeared on the deck. She released his hand and backed up a step, the move as telling as the sudden dip of her gaze and the blush in her cheeks. So much for being at ease in front of the crew...

'You know it doesn't matter how many times I see this sight,' Anya said as she approached, the bosun far more interested in watching the whales than what they had or hadn't been doing. 'I still struggle to tear my gaze away.'

'They're mesmerising,' Maria murmured, looking decidedly uncomfortable as she toyed with the straw in her drink.

'Any idea when we'll get to Gabo?' he asked, drawing Anya's attention his way.

'Captain says we should arrive well before dusk.'

'Great. Can I steal the RIB again, take a trip out to the island?'

'If the weather permits, sure. Just gotta keep an eye on the conditions, it can get pretty hairy around the island quite quickly if the winds pick up.'

'Yeah, I remember, thanks.'

'No worries.' With a friendly smile and one last look at the whales she moved on.

'Are you okay?' he said as soon as Anya was out of earshot.

Maria rubbed the back of her neck. 'Yeah. Sorry. I know we're all on holiday now and according to Trix no one gives a damn what we're doing, but I just…'

'It makes you uncomfortable.'

'Yeah.'

After everything she'd been through with her ex, the gossip she'd endured in his household, he could understand her not wanting to risk the same here. But the idea she would liken their relationship to that messed-up dynamic…he hated it.

'So how about another private boat trip?'

She blinked up at him in surprise.

'What? You didn't think I was planning a solo boat trip, did you?'

'I didn't know what to think.'

'How about thinking private island tour with a Chef Rio picnic?'

'I…' Her cheeks warmed as her mouth hung open, her eyes racing with so much.

'Unless you have something else you'd rather be doing?'

'No.' She licked her cocktail-laced lips. 'Of course not.'

'Then it's a date.'

And pressing a swift kiss to her brow, he left before she could think to back out…

* * *

Wild and remote, Gabo Island gave Maria the shivers.

This was the island Tim thought she'd *love*…?

Sure, the rugged coastline—with its pink granite cliffs and dense green scrub—had a certain raw appeal, but it wasn't for her. It was too isolated, too exposed—too lonely. The towering pink lighthouse on the headland was the only sign of man, and even then it served as a warning to passing ships to steer clear after so many had met their end there.

'You ready to go?'

She turned to find the man himself behind her, two large bags in hand. She hadn't seen him since her cocktail-infused PDA and her bonkers jealousy over whales of all things. She totally blamed the drink. Not the man standing before her in a fresh Henley shirt and cargos, looking fit to play model for some swanky fashion designer, not private tour guide to her.

'Y-yeah.'

'You don't sound so certain.'

'I'm just struggling to see the appeal…' She gestured to the island, making clear she meant *it*, not him. Like he could *ever* possibly think she meant *him*. Fool. 'Deadly island? Luxury yacht? You sure you don't want to stay on board and join the others in their impromptu karaoke night?'

'Do I look like the karaoke kind?'

'I don't know… I reckon you could bang out an awesome Tina Turner.'

'Now I definitely know you're joking.'

She laughed, already imagining it in her mind's eye. 'I'd pay to see it.'

'Never going to happen. Though if you'd rather spend the evening with the crew over me and the picnic Chef Rio has prepared…'

Well, when he put it like that…

'I'm good, let's go.'

He grinned his approval. 'Just tell me you've got something warmer to throw on later?'

He cast his gaze over her and her skin fizzed, her vest and jeans suddenly stifling.

'Anya told me to pack a bag—' she puffed out '—said we might get a little wet on the crossing.'

'It's possible, though I've seen the sea a lot worse.'

'Not what I want to hear,' she said, her body chilling just as quickly. 'Not when Russell's been filling me in on the numerous ships this island has claimed.'

'Cheers, Russell… But you trust me, right?'

She gave an affirming hum, realising just how much she meant it.

'Come on then.'

'You've got the radio just in case…?'

'Yes, I've got the radio.'

'And the weather is good?'

'The weather is good.'

'But it will be getting dark soon.'

'And that's when the real fun starts.'

'The fun?' She squinted at him. Was he joking, flirting, promising a repeat of that morning...?

'Does it beat seeing the whales this afternoon?'

His eyes twinkled like the ocean. 'I'll leave you to be the judge of that... Come on.'

He loaded up the RIB and helped her aboard the rocking vessel, keeping hold until she was safely seated at the rear, his care and attention as thrilling as his touch.

'Thanks.'

His smile was so tender, so... *Damn those cocktails!*

Though she wasn't drunk. Unless being drunk on a man was a thing?

'No problem.'

She pulled her bag onto her lap and watched as he set the boat in motion. His muscles flexing beneath his pale T, those capable hands knowing just what to do...whether they were working the boat or—

He caught her eye, his smirk sizzling. 'You shouldn't be watching me, you should be watching them.'

He motioned towards the island and she turned, her sheepish laugh fading as she took in the flurry of activity. Seals—so many seals! Some lounging lazily on the great pink boulders at the base of the lighthouse while others dived and frolicked in the surging waves...

'They look so happy!'

He grinned back at her. 'So do you.'

He was right. A ridiculous grin stretched across her face—one she hadn't worn in so long, but today it just kept on coming. Her shoulders didn't feel so bunched either. Nature's magic. Or Tim's.

Not something you wanna debate...

Though it was there, still pressing on her mind as he moored the RIB in the small jetty and they hauled their belongings ashore.

'Do you want to eat now, or fancy a tour first?'

'Tour,' she said without hesitation, eager to see what made this island so special—to him, his family. Ellie, too.

Eager to focus on something other than her racing thoughts too.

Don't you mean your feelings?

Over the next hour, he showed her everything there was to see, weaving in stories from his previous visits. How Sasha had picked wildflowers to make a posy for the small picket-fenced cemetery, its three weathered graves so old their inscriptions were illegible, but she'd wanted to give them something nice. How she'd grazed her knee at the stone monument honouring those lost in the 1853 wreck of the ship *Monumental City*, the very tragedy that had led to the lighthouse's construction—yet still insisted on climbing it to the very top.

Maria eyed the lighthouse in the distance. 'That's some climb.'

'One hundred and ninety-six steps. Believe me, I felt every one. But Sasha loved it—especially when she could tell her friends she'd climbed to the very top of the second tallest lighthouse in Australia.'

'What about the tallest?'

'That was the next year.'

She chuckled. 'Quite the little adventurer.'

'She was. Still is. I'll have to tell her that they've turned the Assistant Lightkeeper's Cottage into a holiday let now…'

'A holiday let?'

'You don't look convinced?'

'I guess if you like your solitude, it's perfect.'

Because they hadn't seen another soul. Though the lighthouse keeper had to be around somewhere. And Tim assured her that when the weather was good, the place would often have visitors passing through.

'I don't know,' he said. 'In a world that's forever changing, there's something quite reassuring about a place that stays the same. A place where you can step away from the noise, let go of the pressures in the real world, and just appreciate it for its natural beauty.'

'And enjoy the quiet that isn't quiet at all,' she murmured.

Because between them, the silence was alive with the crash of the waves, the call of the sea-birds, the distant bark of the seals. And the grass...was that frogs? Whatever it was, the land hummed with it.

'Exactly. Ellie and I had busy lives, whether at work or out of it, there were always people around. Coming here was a total break from that.'

'What did she do for work?'

'She was a human rights lawyer.'

Wow, she almost blurted.

'When she wasn't fighting the good fight for the people, she was volunteering at homeless shelters and animal shelters. She had busy feet. Always had to be doing something.'

'She sounds—amazing.'

'Amazing, *and* exhausting.' Though his chuckle was full of fondness for the woman he had lost. 'Coming to places like this made her take a moment, you know.'

Maria nodded, because she could totally see it now. Through his eyes, through theirs—the island's magic unfurling with every memory he'd shared and every step they took. As for Ellie, *hell*, Maria was half in love with the woman herself.

He paused at the edge of a sandy cove and looked back at her, offering out his hand. She took it and together they looked out over the sea and the sun low on the horizon.

He inhaled softly. 'This is the first time I've been since I lost her...'

She looked up at him, all the emotion she'd been trying to suppress surging through her as she realised what this trip meant for him too. 'I'm glad you brought me.'

'So am I.' He gave her a smile, his eyes so full of something...something deep, something that had her throat closing over and her heart in a spin—was that Ellie in his gaze or...?

'We should eat.'

'Eat?' she blurted.

His smile lifted to one side. 'Yeah, you know that thing called food...'

'Sounds good.'

And if she was eating food, she couldn't be devouring him.

Heart, mind *and* soul.

'I think Rio thought the entire crew were coming with us,' Maria said, flopping back on the blanket and palming her stomach with a groan. 'I can't eat another thing.'

'It'll keep,' he said, reaching for the containers to pack away the leftovers and she made a move to help. 'Oh, no, you don't. It's my turn to look after you.'

Her eyes twinkled with the setting sun. 'If you think I'm going to lie here all idle...'

'Do you *ever* let anyone take care of you?'

'Nope.'

She wrapped the cheese and placed it in the cool box, the juice and leftover fruit too. All the while his eyes remained fixed on her, his body unmoving.

'I thought you were packing up,' she said.

'Right now, I'm trying to unpack you.'

She gave an abrupt laugh. 'You've unpacked me enough. No one knows me as well as you—' Her eyes jerked to his, then away just as swiftly as she dived for the bread.

'Is that true?' he said.

'Don't get a big head about it, I'm hardly worth getting all excited about.'

She reached across him to place the bread in the bag he held, and he took it from her, took her hand next. 'Don't say that.'

'I'm only teasing.'

She tried to pull away, but he wouldn't let her go, his hold gentle yet firm. His words too. 'Only you're not.'

Her eyes flickered under his gaze. 'Tim, seriously...'

'You are worth knowing, Maria. You are worth getting excited about. You're...' He ran his thumb along the back her hand and she licked her lips, her mouth parting and drawing his eye. Making

him want, when what she needed was to hear—
'Damn, I want to kiss you. But I don't want you
to think that's all this is...'

A crease formed between her brows as he
reached into her hair.

'You fascinate me, Maria. And the more I get
to know you, the more I like you, and the more
I want—' Her eyes flared and he pulled back,
scared he'd send her running with his need for a
future as much as his need for her in the present.
'You should lie down and watch the cove. Your
night's entertainment is about to begin.'

'My *what*?'

'You'll see.'

This was why he'd brought her so late in the
day. To see the island at dusk. Not to seduce her
and confess his feelings in the process.

But tonight, the appeal of the island had some
serious competition in the woman now lying on
her front beside him. The sunset in her hair, her
eyes, her smile...

Stunning. That was what she was. So why
couldn't she see it?

Her parents. Then Fraser. Her ex. The man who
had chipped away at her for more than a decade,
taking what he'd wanted. The man who now made
his blood boil. Not since Ellie and her diagnosis
had he felt such anger. And the more he thought
of him and what he'd done, the more...

'You shouldn't be watching me—you should be watching them.'

His laugh fractured the sudden tension in his frame. 'Using my words against me.'

'There are whales…' She gestured towards the sea as a massive tail slipped beneath the surface. 'And oh, my God…' She pushed up off the ground. 'Are they—*dolphins*?'

It took him a delayed second to switch from the beauty in her face to the beauty in the ocean. And as much as the pod of dolphins made for a stunning sight, his eyes kept drifting to the one beside him.

He knew which one he'd choose, again and again and again.

CHAPTER THIRTEEN

WITH THE PICNIC packed away, the sun a teeny-tiny sliver on the horizon and the dolphins no longer around, Maria figured it had to be time to go. Especially with the sudden chill in the air and the breeze that had picked up since their arrival on the island.

But she had to admit, there was something special and intimate about being hunkered down on the grassy bank with Tim, a blanket drawn over them both, his body heat as warm as it was provocative.

'Do you—'

A sudden gust snatched at the blanket, cutting her off, and Tim swiftly clamped it back down.

'Okay, I think that's a sign for us to—'

'Shh,' he hushed against her ear. 'Look.'

She peered through the darkness at the waves rolling ashore. Nothing. 'I don't—' And then she saw it, a shifting shadow in the surface of the water. 'Is that…'

He nodded and with a break of foam, a sleek black-and-white body popped up.

'Oh!' she gasped, pressing a hand to her mouth as the little penguin found its feet on the sand, its waddle both cute and hilarious and tickling at her stomach. She scoured the shoreline looking for more, remembering how she'd once taken Fae as a kid to see the fairy penguins landing in St Kilda and how they'd come in droves.

A few minutes passed and nothing. He couldn't be on his own—surely. But then the entire surf came alive, a flurry of black-and-white bodies appearing as if on cue.

Wow! Out they popped, their flippers splayed, some landing gracefully and shaking off the spray, while others tumbled and skidded before they found their feet. The air was filled with chatter as they gathered on the shore before dashing to their burrows and their waiting young.

'Honey, I'm home!' she murmured, and Tim turned to smile at her.

'Can you imagine, all day swimming at sea to come home and have to sick up what you caught for your kids?'

'Way to spoil the moment.'

'Sorry,' he murmured, pressing a kiss to her hair. 'I'll be quiet now.'

She hummed her approval, her own words lost in the thrill of having his mouth so close. Torn between kissing him and the latest charge of penguins disappearing into the hummocky dunes, some coming quite close to where they lay.

'I thought sunrise at Refuge Cove was special, but this…' Then she saw a stray little fella left behind. 'Oh, no, why didn't he leave with the others?'

'He's probably waiting for his mate on the next raft.'

'You think?'

'Just wait…' He gestured as a new wave arrived and, sure enough, the little loner was no longer alone. With the rising cacophony of calls, he came together with another, their waddle as excited and as giddy as Maria now felt.

'Oh, my goodness, that is just….' *Sweet heavens*, she felt like crying. First whales, now penguins. What was wrong with her? 'I can't believe I'm getting all emotional over birds.'

'Or maybe it's the sentiment?' he said softly.

And of course, he'd think that after her foolish statement with the whales and the jealousy… *He's not wrong though, is he?*

'If it makes you feel better, I'd wait for you too.' *Oh, my God.*

He was teasing her, his eyes danced with it, but her head, her heart…

She forced a laugh. 'Who says I wouldn't beat you home?'

Home? She was supposed to be making light of his tease. Instead, her words hit hard. Because a home with this man in it...the idea of it...it was the stuff dreams were made of. And she'd quit dreaming years ago. Or so she'd thought.

He gave a low chuckle. 'Fair point.'

They cosied back down and watched more of the penguins come ashore, wave after wave arriving until the groups became smaller, the sounds on land growing with their homecoming...

'We should get back to the yacht,' Tim said, easing onto his side and stroking her hair over her shoulder. His touch the cure to every panicked thought.

'Or we could stay here?' she said, rolling onto her back to meet his eye. Her previous desire to return to the yacht taken out by the desire to live in this moment now—to dream a little longer.

'And have Trix think I've kidnapped you— you're okay, thanks.'

She gave a hushed laugh. 'I think she'd encourage you to do just that.'

'Really?'

'Oh, yeah, Trix is all for you having your wicked way with me.'

'She *is*?'

'She already has us moving in together—on board, I mean!'

She swallowed. *Watch what you're saying!*

'Sounds good to me...' and then he frowned. 'But you don't want to?'

Want? That room, that luxury, *him.* Always, *him.* 'It's your bed.'

'And?' His mouth twisted with amusement. 'You shared your bed with me, remember.'

'That wasn't premeditated.'

'And this is?'

She didn't get a chance to answer as his mouth closed over hers, soft and tantalising, the lightest sweep of his tongue, and everything about her cried out for more. 'That's a dirty trick.'

'Are you complaining?'

She forked her fingers through his hair and kissed him back. Wanting, needing, pleading… but fearing it too.

Because the more he gave, the more she wanted.

And the more she dared to dream it was possible.

Tim felt the entire world shift and settle around them as she curved her body into his, her kiss turning hungry, desperate, matching him breath for breath.

'Maria,' he groaned against her lips, his hands raking down her sides and slipping beneath her sweater. He palmed the curve of her spine, pressed her closer, wanting—*needing* to feel every inch of her. 'What are you doing to me?'

'The same as what you're doing to me.'

Damn, he hoped so.

Could he really be so lucky as to fall in love twice in one lifetime?

Love—was that what this was?

The world shifted again, only this time he felt the energy shift in the air itself. A chilling gust broke through their heated haven and she stiffened against him, her nails clawing into his shoulder as they looked up at the sky. Ominous clouds moved towards them, drowning out the stars in the distance—a *storm*?

Another sharp gust sent sand skittering across the ground and he pulled her close again, shielding her from the swirling onslaught. Amidst the sound of the island, the muffled crackle of the radio reached him from the bag. He cursed.

'Is that…' Maria started.

'The radio, yeah.'

He had no idea how long it had been going off, between the noise all around and the heat of their kiss…

He twisted to grab the bag, tugging it open.

'Mr Campbell, this is *Celeste*,' came Captain Kali's voice. 'We need you to respond asap. Mr Campbell, can you hear us?'

He snatched it up. 'Captain. It's Tim. We can hear you.'

'Mr Campbell, it's good to hear your voice! We have a cold weather front moving in fast. The crossing isn't safe in these conditions—you need to hold tight and find cover. Hopefully, it'll sweep on through. We'll reassess in an hour. Keep the radio close.'

Captain Kali might as well have said, *Don't ignore me next time.*

'Copy that.' He kept his cool as Maria stared up at him, wide-eyed and pale. 'Come on.'

He stood, clipping the radio to the outside of the bag and hauling her to her feet.

'We need to get to the lighthouse,' he said, gathering up the rest of their things while she did the same. 'We can find cover there.'

Switching on the lantern he'd brought, he took her hand just as a fat raindrop hit the ground, followed by another...

'Best hurry.' He urged her into a run as another drop hit, then another. Before long, they were being attacked from all sides, wind, rain, sand, all of it obscuring the white trail to the lighthouse.

'It's not far!' he shouted, keeping a tight hold of her hand, the beam of the lighthouse as much an aid to them as the ships in the sea now.

It was less than a two-kilometre dash, they could do it in ten if they picked up the pace.

Finally, the dry-stone wall that marked the boundary to the light station finally came into view and he hurried through the gate, heading for the cottage straight ahead. There was no sign of life, just a solitary courtesy light switched on beside the door. He tucked her into the porch and knocked, knocked again.

'Hello!'

No answer.

He tried the door.

Locked.

He scanned the area, the property to his right looked just as shut down. 'Stay here, I'm going to find the keeper.'

'I'll come with you—'

'No, stay sheltered, look after our stuff.' He gave her his bags. 'I won't be long.'

Maria watched him go, her heart in her mouth as the weather closed in around her, relentless even beneath the porch. In no way did this feel like a passing threat.

She gathered the bags to her chest and pressed herself back against the door, squeezing her eyes shut. All the while praying it quit at wind and rain because if the heavens threw thunder and lightning into the mix she feared she might cry.

Captain Kali's voice crackled up to her and her eyes slammed open—the radio!

She dropped all but the bag with it attached and tugged it free, fumbling over the button to respond. 'H-hello? Captain Kali?'

'Maria, is that you?'

'Y-yes.'

'Have you found shelter?'

'We're at—at the lighthouse.'

'That's good. There's a storm rolling in and

we can't hold position. We're moving the yacht to safer waters, we'll return just as soon as it is safe to do so.'

She knew it. *Freaking* knew it.

'Maria, do you copy? Maria?'

She licked her lips, took a shallow breath. 'Yes, we copy.'

'Stay safe, *Celeste* out.'

She gripped the radio to her chest, closed her eyes against the dark.

It's going to be okay, everything will be okay, it's just a bit of bad weather...just—

'I've got a key!'

Her eyes shot open—*Tim.*

He appeared by the light of his lantern, his drenched hair sticking to his face, his clothes like a second skin. He blinked away the droplets clinging to his lashes as he looked down at her, concern etched in every sweet line of his face. Never had she been happier to see someone. She wanted to leap into his arms but she couldn't even move.

'You okay?'

She clenched her jaw. Nodded. His eyes hesitated over her face, his concern still blazing as he unlocked the door and urged her in. He tossed their belongings inside and swept the lantern around. The room was basic but functional. A sofa, a fire, a wooden sideboard and a lamp. She slid off her shoes and moved to switch it on.

'There's no power to the cottage.'

'No p-p-power...' Her teeth chattered. 'How come?'

'They're in the middle of some critical infrastructure work, but the keeper says we're welcome to use the fire and anything else we need.'

'O-okay. Captain Kali radioed while you were gone.'

'What did she say?'

'She...she said a storm was coming and they needed to move to safer water.' Maria tried to push out the fear as she forced herself to relay everything Kali had told her. 'She said they'd return when they could.'

'Okay. No worries.'

'No *worries*?'

'It'll be okay, Maria, honestly.'

She tried to nod but her head refused to move, everything about her was drawn tight. Her body chilled to the bone. A storm. A *freaking* storm on an island as exposed as this. Never mind dreams, this was the stuff of nightmares. For her at any rate.

'The keeper says there are candles and lanterns in the sideboard, wood for a fire and fresh linen that we can help ourselves to.'

He slipped into action while he spoke, finding the lanterns and the candles, lighting a couple before turning his attention to the fire in the grate. All the while she stood rooted, shivering in place. The wind was howling, the shuttered windows clattering, the rain beating wild against the walls…

'Do you want to take the lantern and see if you can find towels and some blankets?'

Did she want to…

'Maria?' He paused before the fire he was building to peer at her and cursed, shot to his feet. He was across the room in a heartbeat, his hands hot and sure on her arms. 'What is it?'

She shook her head.

'Tell me.' His thumbs stroked her through her clothing, the gentle pressure a reassuring hit of both heat and strength.

'I… I don't like thunderstorms,' she whispered. 'They terrify me.'

His frown deepened. 'You're serious?'

She nodded. 'D-don't look so sh-shocked.'

'I'm just surprised…'

'W-why?'

'Because last night with Cherry, you were fear-less.'

'Last n-night, the heavens weren't cr-crashing down on us.'

'And they're not crashing down on us now… Oh, baby, come here…' He pulled her into his arms, kissed her hair, his 'baby' echoing through her, warm and as soothing as any lullaby. 'It's going to be fine. I promise. Keepers have sur-vived here for well over a century, the building we're in has stood for all of that. You'll be fine, I promise.'

She nodded against his chest, feeling tiny and weak. And she hated being weak. Fraser had made her feel weak and she'd sworn she'd never feel like that again. Or let another see her like so. But with the rain hammering, the wind howling, the waves crashing against the rocks and the threat of an impending storm, she was crumbling, and she couldn't stop it.

'You're frozen. We need to get you out of these clothes.'

She nodded as he led her from the room with the lantern, pushing open doors and looking in cupboards, gathering up everything they could use—towels, pillows, blankets.

'I'll get the fire going while you get yourself dry, okay?'

Numb, she took the towel and blanket he offered her and watched while he built the fire. It flickered to life and he got to his feet, brushing off his hands and pulling off his T. He turned to find her in the same position. Still clothed. Still wet. Still stunned.

His eyes narrowed, his jaw pulsing as he let his T-shirt drop to the floor, then he closed the distance between them. Slow this time. Tentative. He raised his hands to her face, stroking away the wet strands from her eyes, her cheeks, her mouth...

'Do you want me to help you?'

She swallowed, her nod as juddery as her insides felt.

'Okay.'

He drew her to the space before the fire, the concern in his gaze burning with the flames that danced in his depths. And she focused on those as he took the blanket and the towel from her trembling hands.

'Arms up, baby girl.'

She did as he bade, his eyes staying fixed on hers as he peeled her sweater over her head, her T-shirt too. Each item hitting the floor as his half-naked body came ever closer.

'It's going to be okay,' he murmured. 'I've got you.'

She nodded, her eyes drifting to his chest. The beauty before her soothing away the harsh reality beyond the walls, the noise drowned out by the thudding of her heart and the chill raced away by the fever in her blood.

His mouth twitched. 'What did you say?'

She hadn't said anything—had she?

'It sounded like "Refuge Cove".'

She nipped her lip as a tremor ran through her. Though this time she couldn't be sure it was fear or the desire to reach out and touch what was tantalisingly close.

'I was likening you to the cove…its beauty and its power to make you forget…'

'Forget?'

She looked up into his eyes, the smallest of nods. 'Forget how cruel life can be...'

And she wasn't just talking about the cruelty of the storm now, she was talking about him as a man with the power to make her feel again, the power to make her hurt again...

But in that moment, she didn't care. She lifted her palms to his chest, felt his body tighten and pulse beneath her touch.

'Make me forget.' Her voice was no more than a husky whisper. 'Please.'

His eyes dipped to her lips, a moment's hesitation and then his arms came around her, setting her skin alight as his mouth came down on hers. Hard and punishing, in all the best ways. More powerful than any storm could be—more powerful than any *man* had any right to be.

He unhooked her bra and swept it from her shoulders, popped the button on her jeans. And then he was on his knees, peeling the wet denim down her thighs. His hands hot, his kisses hotter.

She gripped his shoulders as he tugged each leg free. Stripped her socks too. He teased kisses over one thigh, then the other, smoothed his hands up the back of her legs, his fingers curling into the waistband of her knickers. He pressed a kiss to the lace and she gasped, her hands launching to his hair. He looked up, caught her eye, the fire in the grate nothing on the look in his eyes as he pressed another slow kiss to her sweet spot, teasing it through the lace with his tongue.

'Tim!' She rocked against the pressure, his eyes deliciously intense on hers and staying as he eased the lace down, letting it fall from her knees to the floor as he cupped her behind and brought her to his mouth. His tongue flicked across her throbbing clitoris, and her knees buckled, his hands taking her weight and holding her in place.

'You are beautiful,' he said against her skin. 'You are safe.' His tongue rolled over her. 'I've got you.'

He sucked back over the sensitised nub and she cried out, her fingers clawing, her stomach contracting.

'That's it, baby, let me catch you.' He slid his fingers between her folds, filling her as he teased her with his tongue, driving her to the brink so quickly she couldn't catch her breath. She couldn't—she couldn't…

Her orgasm hit with the first strike of lightning and she cried out his name as the stark white light slashed through the shutters.

'I've got you.' He held her steady against his mouth, took every wave her body offered up, stayed until her limbs had softened, and her breaths had slowed. He stood, holding her against him in one arm while he threw a blanket over the sofa, then he set her down upon it.

'I still need you,' she murmured as he straightened, uncaring of what she was saying, what she was admitting, 'Please.'

His throat bobbed, every exposed muscle in his body straining as he unbuttoned his jeans and slid them off with his underwear.

Naked and hers.

The thought pierced her brain, caught at her heart as he lowered himself over her. Desire blazing in his gaze as he stroked his hand down her side, cupping her knee to raise it to his lips. He kissed it softly, hooking it over his shoulder as his fingers dipped to caress her. Easing her back to the brink, until she was panting and desperate and couldn't take much more.

'Please, Tim.'

He was so close, he just needed to…

'Make love to me.'

And then he cursed, the tension in his face dialling up a gear as he froze and looked away.

'What's wrong?'

He dragged in a ragged breath. What had she done? What had she said? Oh, God, make *love*! She combed her fingers into his hair, rested her palms against his cheeks as she forced him back to face her. The tortured look in his eyes tearing her heart in two. Was it Ellie?

Her thighs slackened around him.

'I can't,' he said through his teeth. 'We don't have any protection.'

Never had she been more relieved. And with

that came a spark of terror. She licked her lips. 'It's okay.'

His brows drew together. 'How?'

'I'm on the pill. I'm safe. I got tested after Fraser…'

There'd been no one else *since* Fraser—the meaning of that was enough to make the fresh wriggle in her gut worm its way deeper.

'I assume you're…'

He nodded. 'But are you sure?'

Sure? She kissed him until the wriggle quit. 'Yes.'

With a low groan, he rose up over her, his eyes piercing hers as she splayed her hands against his chest and lowered her gaze. She marvelled at every honed muscle accentuated by the light of the fire, all the way to where their bodies met, *almost* melded.

'Are you sure?' Another husky rasp, his body straining to take what it so evidently needed, but he was still Tim, determined to put her needs first.

Which was why she knew this was right. That this was what she wanted. That she, heaven forbid, would always want this.

She let her eyes drift back to his and she nodded, rolling her hips as he rocked his, each delicious inch claiming her heart as much as her body. There was no going back. She knew that now. And she surrendered to it. Moving with him as he filled her, their tempo building as fierce as the crashing weather outside.

They cried their release as the roll of thunder hit and she quivered in his hold.

'I've got you, baby girl.' He kissed her throat, her cheek, her lips. 'I've got you.'

'I know.'

Because she did know. He had her heart, soul and mind, and it made her quiver even more because there wasn't a damn thing she could do about it...

Not in the now, not until she could get away from him and then she'd run. As fast as her legs could take her. And keep on running until common sense prevailed and her life was safe and contained and all about her and Fae once more.

'I know,' she repeated quietly. 'I know.'

CHAPTER FOURTEEN

TIM HAD NO idea what time it was, or how long it had been since the thunderstorm had quit its rumble overhead. Their lovemaking had blended effortlessly into sleep into lovemaking into sleep again. Over and over like some fevered dream, only it was very much real, and reality would soon come calling. The light creeping through the slits in the shutters told him to get the radio back on. Though he had no desire to move. Not yet.

Not with her body entwined with his on the sofa, her fingers caressing his chest beneath the blanket he'd pulled up over them. She was sated, relaxed, no trace of the tension the storm had caused, but he couldn't forget it.

She'd been so pale, so lost in her fear...paralysed by it, too.

'Have you always been afraid of thunderstorms?' he asked, his eyes on the ceiling but his entire focus on her and the way her breath sighed through her.

'No.'

'Did something happen?'

'You don't want to hear about this.'

'I wouldn't ask if I didn't want to know.'

She looked up at him, wet her lips then tucked herself in deeper against his chest.

'When I was about seven, I ran away from home.' Her arm tightened around his waist... or was that him drawing her closer? 'I told you we never had any money, so things like uniform were always a trigger for a fight. I'd outgrown my school shoes but my parents refused to buy me new ones. Then one day the teacher called them up on it, she'd noticed they were hurting me... You can imagine how that went down. My father was humiliated, blamed me for telling tales.' She gave a bitter laugh. 'Like I'd want anyone to know that truth. Anyway, after he was done taking out his temper on me, they locked me in my room. I just figured, if I wasn't around any more, things would be so much better for everyone. I didn't get far. The weather turned nasty and I hid in the playground. They had this old helter-skelter and I hid in its base. I had no idea whether I was safe there, I was just petrified of the storm and didn't dare move. A mother with her kid found me there the next morning, they took me to the police.'

'And your parents?' he forced out, the words hard to form with the anger rolling through him.

'They were livid. Turned out running away only made it worse. I never tried it again.'

He cursed and hugged her tight. Kissed her hair, breathed in her scent, her warmth, her safe and reassuring presence in the now.

'The police *never* should have let you go back.'

'I didn't tell them what had happened. I didn't speak for days. Mum and Dad made up some excuse about how they'd thought I was with a friend. And who would have me anyway? There were no aunts or uncles or grandparents to take me away. The neighbours gave us a wide berth because of how they were, and their kids avoided me too.'

'No wonder you were so desperate to leave.'

Leave and land herself in bigger bother with just as big a piece of scum.

He wanted to rewrite her past, protect her from it all, no matter how impossible a wish it was.

'There was this one teacher though, Miss Smith, she was real sweet. Used to bring me books and treats, tried to include me, but then her mother got sick and she had to leave. I learnt pretty quickly not to get attached again.'

'Until Fraser?' Just saying the name sent fire up his throat, a searing mix of anger and pain.

'And look how well that turned out...'

She pressed up off his chest. 'I'm going to try out the shower.'

Was that code for give me space? Literally pushing him away too.

She slipped out from under the blanket and stood. The cool slivers of dawn painted her naked body alabaster, her hair almost black as it tumbled down her back—wild from sleep, even wilder from his touch.

She turned to eye him over her shoulder.

'You wanna join me…it might be warmer with two.'

He cracked a grin—relief, desire, and something far deeper, far more instinctive surging through him.

He got to his feet and lifted her into his arms, treasuring her laugh. 'Best idea I've heard all day.'

It's a fling. Just a fling. A sizzling, mind-altering, fear-beating fling.

But even as she told herself the words she could feel herself wanting to deny it. Make it into more. The same old dream she'd had with Fraser, for a future and a happy ever after, trying to make its way back in. But she'd been young and naive enough to believe in it back then. She knew better now.

She knew to make the most of the fun and walk away when done.

And combing her hands through his hair as he travelled kisses down her body, the shower raining over them, she was certainly making the most of the fun…

'I can't get enough of you.'

His words, murmured against her navel, clutched

at her heart, and she bit down on her lip—forcing them away, forcing his head down further too.

They mean nothing. They're just words. Empty promises gifted in the moment.

He chuckled, low and slow. 'Impatient, baby girl.'

Impatient to make him stop speaking—yes!

She couldn't listen to it. She couldn't believe it. But everything about Tim was trustworthy, and that made everything he said all the more dangerous. As for the endearment—baby girl—her entire body sighed.

'Yes! We have a radio to turn back on!'

'Ah, the radio…' he circled her clitoris with his thumb '… I think there's something more pressing to turn on this second.'

Her body trembled, his words and his skilled caress taking her to the precipice faster than she could think—

'Tim!' She flung her hands to his shoulders, her nails biting into his lats as her entire body rocked against his touch. 'Get up here.'

'Your wish is my command.' He was on his feet, turning her into the wall as he effortlessly claimed her, his growl as guttural as her cry. She palmed the cold tiles as he drove her to the edge with him. Never had she climaxed so easily or so frequently, not even with Fraser.

But then he wasn't Fraser, came the untimely reminder.

He was so much more.

And therein lay the bigger problem—Fraser hadn't been half the man Tim was proving to be, and Fraser had broken her. Dismantled her confidence, her autonomy, her independence and her worth. Until she'd become a mere shell of her former self.

It had taken four years to get to where she was now. Better. Stronger for what she'd been through. And Tim was all about lifting her up, making her into more, offering up his honesty and his care too. How could she possibly keep a lid on how he made her feel?

But if Fraser had broken her, heaven knew what Tim could do, given half a chance...

And it was that thought that pierced through her post-orgasm haze, sending goosebumps rife across her body.

'Do you hear that?' he murmured in her ear.

'Hear what?'

She twisted in his arms, her eyes shooting to the open door as above the noise of the shower, the continued rain and wind outside, there was an intermittent knocking...a rap of knuckles on wood.

'Hello!'

Her eyes widened at the stranger's voice. 'Is that—?'

'The keeper. Gotta be.' He scrambled out of the shower. 'I'll deal with him.'

He grabbed a towel and wrapped it around his waist, almost losing his footing on the wet wooden floor and a giggle burst through her. 'Easy, tiger.'

He smacked a kiss on her lips and legged it out. She laughed after him, the happy bubble swiftly bursting as she realised just how easily he made her forget where her head had been. Where it still should be. In the land of caution.

She took a deep breath, pushing out her thoughts and her feelings that all revolved around him, and stepped out of the shower. Through the closed door she could make out the rumble of voices, indistinct but ongoing.

Raking her fingers through her hair, she tried to tame every tangle, doing the same with her thoughts too, but it was no use, the end result was just as messy, just as confused, just as—stop!

She walked up to the mirror and gripped the sink. Lifted her gaze to her reflection and saw a woman she didn't recognise looking back at her.

So much colour in her cheeks, her eyes so bright and body flushed pink. The telltale trail of marks from their lovemaking—no, not lovemaking—sex.

That was what Trix would call it.

And so should she.

Sex. A fling. Finite!

'No one gets hurt,' she whispered, 'least of all you.'

'Maria!'

She looked to the door. 'Yes?'

'Breakfast is served.'

Breakfast?

She wrapped a towel around her body and padded out of the room. Coffee? She could smell *coffee!*

She followed the scent to the kitchen and found him sat at a feast-laden table, her eyes bugging out over the food as much as him dressed in fresh lounge pants and a T she didn't recognise.

'He brought you clothes, too,' Tim said, guessing at her thoughts.

'He did?'

'The T-shirt will likely drown you but the bottoms have a drawstring waist so you should be good.'

'That's very sweet of him, and this…' She took in the array of food—honey, jam, butter, fruit, a giant loaf, a carton of milk, a cafetière of coffee *and* a box of mainstream cereal. 'This is amazing.'

'The bread's freshly baked too, the keeper's own recipe. The rest are staples from his stores. He says to shout if we need any more.'

'Any more?' She slid onto a wooden chair and poured herself a coffee. 'There's enough to feed us twice over.'

'That's what I said. I think even Rio would be impressed.'

She popped a piece of bread in her mouth, having slathered it in honey, and moaned. 'Oh yes, Rio would wholeheartedly approve.'

It was utterly delicious. And the coffee— heaven in a cup!

'Okay, so keep that sweet sensation in mind as I tell you the bad news.'

She swallowed. 'The *bad* news?'

'He heard from Captain Kali this morning, *Celeste* isn't coming back any time soon.'

'She *isn't*?'

The blood seeped from her face as the bread got stuck somewhere between her tonsils and her tensed-up stomach.

'The conditions are too choppy. The tender won't be leaving the jetty for another couple of days at least.'

'A couple of days…?' she repeated softly.

'Afraid so.'

She forced down the food with coffee. 'What are we going to do?'

'We could make the most of our extended stay…a change up to our vacation?' The spark in his eyes lit a fire in her stomach, and she pressed a hand to it. Now was not the time to be thrilled by him, now was the time to get the hell out, before…

'*Your* vacation—it was supposed to be a work trip for me, remember.'

'A trip you've already been paid for in full, so now you can afford the extended holiday. The keeper assured me we were welcome, said he'll even launder our clothes if need be.'

She licked her lips. 'I can't just stay here. I have a job to get back to. I have Fae…she's going to worry.'

'Trix will get a message to Fae. And surely Mickey can survive without you for a day or two.'

'Not without Trix as a backup he can't.'

'He must have other staff that can fill in. They're doing so now, aren't they?'

'They've already covered for me enough.'

Tim leaned back in his seat, his eyes narrowing. 'Okay.'

Okay. Nothing was okay. She was trapped here, on an island with a man she couldn't, wouldn't, *feared* she was already in love with.

'There's also the opportunity to get a flight off the island before then.'

'A flight?'

He nodded, his mouth forming a grim line. Had he guessed at her panic? Had he sussed it had nothing to do with Mickey and everything to do with him?

'The conditions should allow for an air transfer to Merimbula as soon as tomorrow morning.'

'Merimbula?'

'Yes. And from there we can fly to Melbourne.'

'And you—you can sort that?'

'The keeper can arrange the flight for us, and

from Merimbula, my jet can get us back to Melbourne.'

'Your…' she swallowed '…*jet*?'

He nodded like it was an entirely normal thing to have on hand.

'When you say *your*, you don't mean your *your*, do you?'

'I don't fly it, if that's what you mean, my piloting skills are strictly limited to the water.'

'I meant the jet. Is it yours?'

'Yes. Why?'

Yes. Why, Maria? You already knew he was loaded, why be surprised at this tiny added detail?

But how easy it had been to forget how very different they were when they were stuck on a remote island, cut off from their realities. Realities she clung to now as she used them to bolster her defences.

'And you're happy to use it to fly me back to Melbourne?'

'In truth, I'd fly you anywhere you wanted to go.'

Her heart slammed against her ribs, her eyes flaring as she choked in protest.

'I mean it, Maria. Name a place and I'd take you tomorrow. Pick one of the places off that wall of yours and have at it.'

Her stomach fizzed over with her heart. 'You're crazy.'

'I'm not crazy.'

He reached for her hand across the table and she drew back, folding her arms as she stared at him. Shock and something else she didn't want to acknowledge stealing her voice and her appetite.

'I want to spend more time with you.' He frowned. 'I thought, after everything, you might want that too?'

Against all her better judgement, yes.

'I know you're worried about Fae, but don't you think what we have deserves a chance at something more? And you've always wanted to travel, I can give you that, I can give you *and* Fae that.'

'Not everyone can just up and leave when they feel like it, Tim.'

They had jobs, responsibilities...

She pushed away from the table, strode to the window. Her gaze on the rolling sea outside but her mind on the storm within.

'You're asking me to let you into our lives, to risk upending what we've built together, all for the sake of a fling?'

'Not for the sake of a fling, no. I'm asking you to take a chance on forever, Maria.'

His words were dancing all over her heart, firing up the flutters, no matter that she'd learned long ago to take such words with a pinch of salt. When would she learn?

'Forever?' she choked out. 'How can you have any faith in forever after Ellie? What you had to-

gether was beautiful and look what happened…
Nothing good lasts forever.'

'And yet it's a risk I'm willing to take. Do you
think knowing what the future had in store would
have stopped me from choosing a life with Ellie?
No, it wouldn't. And I'm doing the same now. I'm
choosing you, Maria.' He came up behind her,
his hand soft on her shoulder as he turned her to
face him. 'I've spent the last seven years with my
life on hold, and I want to live it again. I want to
live it again with you. Please don't give up on us
without giving us a chance.'

'I…' She couldn't say it. Not when every fibre
of her being wanted him, cared for him…*loved*
him? 'I want to go home.' She beat back the rush
of feeling as she lifted her eyes to his. 'Please,
Tim. Take me home.'

His jaw twitched, his eyes burned, a second's
silence, then, 'Okay. If that is what you want, that
is what we'll do.'

Want? No, she didn't want it. She wanted him.
She wanted this. She wanted it all for the rest of
her life, but she'd been a fool to long for forever
once, she wouldn't be that fool again.

'Thank you.'

They didn't speak of it again. Even when she'd
slipped into his arms that night and their mouths
had found each other. They'd made love but it was
quiet. Dampened by the impending end. Tim's

head screamed at him to do something, to say something, to lay his heart bare, but he couldn't. He'd already said enough, and he didn't want to ruin what time they had left, hashing it out, only to get to the same depressing end.

Or worse, have her shut him out entirely.

At least this way, she'd spent the night in his arms.

But with every passing hour he'd felt her withdraw. In the morning, she barely ate, she barely spoke. Her smile reserved for the lighthouse keeper as she thanked him for all that he had done for them. On the transfer from the island, she only spoke when spoken to and with his jet she'd been full of polite praise. But there was no sparkle in her gaze, no playfulness in her wonder, no sign of the woman he had come to love so much in so short a spell.

Even when Connor called to tell them the news that Cherry was out of danger and doing well, she'd said how pleased she was to hear it, that it was a relief, but every word had been weighted with this. With them.

By the time his car pulled up outside Mickey's Bar, Muted Maria was driving him out of his mind.

He understood why she didn't want to rock the carefully curated life she had built with Fae. Why it was so sacred and man-free too. But he knew what they had, and he knew what it could be.

And as much as he didn't want to open himself up to potential heartache in the future, he realised he no longer had a choice. Whether she chose to end it now or he lost her further down the line, the pain would be no more real, no less visceral.

'This was supposed to be a fling,' she said as his driver cut the engine, her voice so quiet he had to strain to hear her. 'No one was supposed to get hurt.'

'I know that, Maria.'

'Then why did you do it?' Her eyes lifted to his, their pain crushing him. 'Asking me for more when you knew I couldn't give it.'

'I didn't ask you to make you feel guilty, I asked you because I hoped you felt the same.'

'It wasn't fair.'

'Life isn't fair. We've both learned that the hard way.' He took her hand in his, grateful when she let him. 'Please, Maria. Don't walk away from this, from me, not yet. Give me time to show you how good we could be together, how good life could be?'

'I *have* a good life. Here with Fae. It's safe and it's ours. Now, please, let me go.'

He stared into her eyes, his heart and soul screaming *No!,* but how could he refuse her?

His driver opened her door and she tugged her bag up off the floor.

'Goodbye Tim.'

And then she was walking away and there

wasn't a damn thing he could do about it. Not if he wanted to respect her wishes.

But what about doing justice to your own?

With a raw curse he slid out after her. 'Maria!'

She paused on the footpath, her shoulders lifting with the smallest of breaths as he came up behind her.

'Maria?'

Slowly she turned, her eyes lifting to his. 'Yes?'

'I know you don't want to hear this, but I also know I'll regret it if I don't say it to you now.'

She swallowed. 'Don't do it, Tim, please d—'

'I *love* you.'

Her mouth fell open, her lashes quivered. 'No. You can't.'

'Why can't I?'

'Because you've known me all of five minutes,' she choked out.

'And? In all my years, I've only met two women who made me feel this way. My wife was one and I will always carry her with me. You're the other and the same will be true whether you walk away from me now or not. I will always carry you here.'

He covered his heart as she gripped her middle. 'You can't use me to replace her.'

He gave a sharp frown. 'That wasn't what—'

'No, because it sounds like it. And I won't be some substitute for your affections.' She threw the words at the ground. 'I won't.'

'How can you even suggest that?'

She was lashing out, he realised, trying to hurt him to get *him* to walk.

Which meant she had to be running scared. And that had to mean she cared.

'You know me, Maria, and in your heart of hearts you know that's not what this is.' Reaching out, he lifted her chin, forcing her to meet his gaze. 'What I feel for you is no less than what I felt for her. But make no mistake, it is different, because you are different. And I *do* love you.'

'Stop saying that. Please just stop!' Her eyes overflowed with her tears as she tugged his hand away. 'Fraser said it, too. *All* the time. How much he loved me. How much he wanted to be with me. And it was all lies. Just lies.'

'Maybe. Or maybe it was the truth and he did love you, but it sure as hell wasn't a healthy kind of love. It's not the kind of love I feel for you. Because nothing would stop me from choosing you. Nothing would stop me from protecting you.'

'I'm not *yours* to protect.'

'My heart disagrees.'

'Tim, please…'

'No, you need to hear this. I'm lucky to have been surrounded by love all of my life. By my family, by Ellie, by Sasha, even Connor, and I want to ensure you never go another day without feeling it too.'

'I do feel it. Fae is the most loving daughter one could ever hope to have.'

'And you can have me, too. I want to build my life around you, Maria. You, Sasha *and* Fae. I can't force you to see the truth in that, but I am asking you to give me the chance to prove it to you. To show you what we could make of life together.'

She shook her head, swiped at her damp cheeks. 'I can't.' She swallowed. 'I can't.'

And then she ran, pushing through the door to the bar and disappearing inside.

He moved to follow but someone stepped out of the shadows, drawing him up short. Fae!

She met his gaze, her eyes so like her mother's shimmering with something. Was that...*sympathy*?

'I'm sorry,' he said, because what else could he say. Fae had made her feelings clear that very first day they'd met, and now he'd brought her mother home in tears, confirming her worst suspicions.

'Me too.'

CHAPTER FIFTEEN

'Mum?'

Maria stiffened. She'd thought she was alone. The bar deserted. Else she'd never have dropped into a chair and sobbed into the table with her head in her arms. The last person she wanted to see her like this was Fae.

She hadn't gone upstairs because—Fae.

She hadn't risked her heart anew because— Fae.

No, that wasn't true. She hadn't risked her heart anew because—this! So, this!

The pain of loving someone, trusting someone, letting them in...

Not that she'd ever truly loved Fraser. She realised that now. Because this was so much more— *Tim* was so much more.

And she'd walked away because she was utterly terrified of being that broken woman again and look at her now. Broken anyway.

'Mum?'

This time Fae's footsteps accompanied her

soft call and, peeling herself off the table, Maria swiped away her tears and turned.

'Darling, what are you doing here? I thought you'd be upstairs getting ready for your shift.'

'You're really asking me what I'm doing here when you're the one sat sobbing?'

She gave a weak smile. 'I'll be okay.'

'You don't look it, and you sure as hell don't sound it.'

'You're right,' she admitted weakly, getting to her feet. 'Can I have a hug?'

She opened her arms and Fae filled them, wrapping her own around her waist and resting her head against Maria's chest.

'I think you should go after him.'

She stiffened. 'Who?'

'You know who I'm talking about.' Fae leaned back to look up at her, her eyes awash with concern. 'I saw you outside together. I heard what he said.'

'You were eavesdropping?'

'Not on purpose. I was coming back from a walk, and I saw him run after you.'

She tucked Fae's head beneath her chin, unable to hold her daughter's gaze while inside her heart was shattering with his replayed words…

I want to build my life around you, Maria.

I love you, Maria.

I've got you, baby girl.

'I didn't want to get in the way,' Fae said quietly.

'You could never be in the way, not ever.'

'Are you in love with him?'

Maria choked on her tears. 'What—why would you say that?'

'Because look at you, Mum. I haven't seen you like this in forever, and even then, your pain was more about your frustrations for me, rather than yourself. This is all about you now.'

She gave a soft huff. 'When did you get so wise?'

'When you were so busy taking care of me you forgot to take care of yourself. But that has to stop, Mum. You need to start living your life for you again. I heard what he said to you. I saw how he looked when you walked away. I may not know much about relationships, and heaven knows, Dad did a total number on you, but I'm not sure walking away from him out there was the right thing to do.'

'You've changed your tune, not two weeks ago you couldn't wait for me to get shot of him.'

'That was before…'

'Before what?'

'Before he fell in love with you.'

Her heart gave a painful beat. 'You shouldn't believe everything you hear.'

'I don't, believe me, but he isn't Dad, Mum. He's nothing like him. Dad was all about himself. Taking what he wanted and dropping what he didn't. He was a liar and a user. Tim is none of those things.'

'You don't even know him, love, how can you possibly say what he is and isn't?'

'Take a look around, Mum. Do you really think Mickey suddenly came up with the money for all this work?'

'Huh?' She blinked, only now noticing the state of the bar. The dust sheets on the tables, the builders' tools stacked in one corner, a fresh 'Closed for Refurb' sign hanging on the door...

'The surveyor that came to the house that morning you left was just the beginning. Mickey's had people in and out for days. He's buzzing with ideas. I asked him what had gotten into him, and he said this guy just rocked up at his office. Asked him about the place, the history, what it meant to Mickey and his family, and then offered to invest. Offered him a deal he couldn't refuse. His time and his money.'

'I don't understand.'

'Tim didn't tell you, did he?'

'Are you saying it was *Tim*? That *he* gave Mickey the money?'

Fae nodded. 'At first, I was mad, I figured he was trying to buy your affections, just like Dad used to. I was going to ring you and warn you, but your phone was out of range. That's when Trix messaged to let us know about the storm. But having heard all that out there... I don't know, Mum. Those weren't the words of a selfish man, wanting to get what he could out of you.'

Maria cursed. 'I can't believe he'd do this. Of all the interfering, manipulative—'

'But that's just it, Mum. I don't think it was about that at all. If it was, he would have told you about his involvement in the bar, used it to convince you to stay instead of walk away.'

'Or did he walk knowing that he'd be back, for the bar, for Mickey, for me?' She cursed, ramming a hand through her hair as she eyed all the work in progress and seeing his mark in every one. Her home wasn't even *hers* any more. Just like her home with Fraser had been all his. *His* choice, *his* money, *his* suffocating presence. 'I can't believe this.'

'Where are you going?'

She hadn't realised she was running until Fae called out after her.

'To have it out with him.'

'He's *not* Dad, Mum!'

'He might as well be and I won't be put in that position. Not again.'

She pulled open the door just as his car started to pull away...

Tim's car came to a screeching halt, his driver's apology drowned out by the thundering beat of his heart. Because there was Maria. Standing in front of his car, her palms pressed to the bonnet, her eyes spearing his through the windscreen.

'What do you want me to do, sir?'

244 CINDERELLA'S FLING WITH THE BILLIONAIRE

'Just hang back.' He unbuckled his seatbelt. 'I'll call when I'm ready for you.'

He pushed open his door.

'How could you?' she hissed.

Not a happy U-turn then…

'How could I what?' he said as he joined her on the pavement.

She gestured to the bar. '*You're* the investor behind Mickey's refurb.'

'The place was in need of a cash injection.'

'And you just took it upon yourself to offer it. Your involvement had nothing to do with *you* sleeping with *me*?'

He scanned the footpath as the odd passerby glanced their way and urged her into a side street, his voice low as he admitted, 'Of course it had something to do with you. Do you honestly think I could see the issues with the building and not do anything about it?'

'The issues with the—' she spluttered, her entire body trembling. 'Why? What the hell is it to you? Mickey's been good to us, the best landlord. He's looked out for us from the day we moved in and you dared to come along and pick at him! Not everyone has the kind of money you do to throw into non-essential maintenance!'

'Non-essential? That damp could make you ill. And it sure as hell isn't good for the building. Mickey *is* a good man, but a good landlord he is not. He's been charging too low a rent for years and the building has suffered because of it. In helping people, he's failed to help himself and safeguard the future of the place. I offered to help him, not just because you're his tenant but because this is his family's legacy, and the idea of him being forced out by some developer looking to make a quick buck further down the line didn't sit right with me. This way, he gets to give the place some TLC, bring it up-to-date, and *choose* when he sells. He gets to retire on his terms.'

'And then what, you take a huge chunk of the sale?'

'No, Maria. If I had my way, I'd walk away with nothing, knowing I've done some good here. But Mickey is a proud man; he doesn't want a handout, he wants a fair deal, and that's what he got. I wasn't about to injure his pride by pushing my own agenda. Now, if you're done taking down *my* pride, I'll be the one to say goodbye this time.'

'Wait!'

He paused.

'Why...why didn't you tell me what you'd done? All that time we spent together and you didn't mention it, not once.'

'You're asking me that after the way you're reacting now?'

'But if you'd told me...if you'd explained...'

'You'd still think the worst, because you can't look past Fraser to the man I am. And while you still see him, I can't—'

'I know you're not Fraser.'

It was a whisper, but it was enough to have him face her full-on. 'Say that again?'

'I know you're not Fraser.'

He pressed his lips together. Swallowed. 'And that terrifies you, doesn't it?'

'Yes.'

'Why, Maria? Tell me, why?'

He could see it in her eyes, but he needed to hear her say it. Yearned for it.

'He broke me. Ripped me apart, and it took me years to piece myself back together again. But you made me realise I never loved him at all. And if someone could hurt me that much without love, the idea of being hurt by someone I do love. The idea of being hurt by you...'

'Maria,' he whispered, his voice raw as he felt her pain, but also hope, hope for a future he'd all but given up on, 'I could never hurt you.'

'You can't know that.' She was trembling, the fear in her eyes unbearable. 'And to be that vulnerable again by choice...'

'It's okay to be vulnerable, Maria. We're all vulnerable in love. Don't you think I feel it too? That when you walked away from me just now my whole world didn't come crashing in...'

'I'm sorry.'

'I don't need you to be sorry, I just need you to see the truth.'

'And the truth is what terrifies me, because

you are everything Fraser wasn't and you're everything I could ever want. Because I do love you Tim, and I know now that no amount of running away is going to change that.'

'Then how about running this way instead?'

He opened his arms to her and a slow smile spread across her face, a fresh well of tears coming too, and then she was in his arms. And as much as he wanted to lose himself in that moment, he knew he had to come totally clean first. 'There's something else you need to know…'

She stiffened in his hold. 'O-okay?'

'I employed a PI to look into Fraser.'

'*What*—why?'

'Why do you think?'

'But Tim, he's firmly in my past.'

'He's also clean as a whistle, but I'll get him Maria, I swear to God, I'll make him pay for—'

She pressed a finger to his lips. 'No. You won't. You taught me to let go of my past and my shame for being the other woman. You taught me to move forward. I've wasted enough of my life thinking of him, and I almost let my history with him ruin my future with you. He's done enough damage, and I don't want to think of him any more.'

'But Maria, what he did—'

'Was wrong. Yes. But karma will catch up with him eventually, and if it doesn't I don't care, because I'm happy. I'm happy because I have you. I know what true love is because of you. And I wouldn't change a thing in my life, because ultimately it gave me Fae and it gave me you. And I am the luckiest woman alive for it all.'

'How can I argue with any of that?'

'You can't.' She cocked one confident brow. 'You can kiss me though?'

'I thought you'd never ask…'

And then he swept her into his arms and kissed her until need threatened to push the boundaries of public decency. 'Now can we go inside so that I can show you just how much?'

'Fae's inside.'

'*Fae* is heading out.' Their heads shot around to find Fae sauntering past, one hand raised in a wave. 'Have fun, kids, don't do anything I wouldn't do.'

He chuckled. 'Does this mean she accepts me now?'

'I think it means she wants me to be happy and right now, she thinks you're the answer to that.'

'I'll always be the answer to that.'

'Cocky, much?'

'Just you wait until we get inside, baby girl. I'll prove it to you again and again if needs be.'

'Promises, promises.'

'And you can trust in every one.'

She searched his gaze as she cupped his cheek. 'I know. And I love you for it.'

'And I love you.'

EPILOGUE

One year later...
London, England.

MARIA HADN'T STOPPED SMILING. From the moment they'd touched down in Heathrow she'd been abuzz with nervous excitement. Today wasn't just about another new city on her bucket list. It was about Tim's daughter, Sasha, and her charity's annual gala.

She'd been primped and polished within an inch of her life. Hair, make-up, nails, dress—she'd barely recognised herself as she'd stepped up to the mirror, the bold red dress skimming over her figure in all the right ways. But she'd recognised herself in Tim's gaze. The familiar desire burning in his depths as he'd stood back and admired her. Just the memory of that look made her quiver now.

'Are you cold?'

His hand pulsed around hers on the back seat of their chauffeured car.

'No.' She met his gaze. 'Far from it.'

'Good, because we have a small detour to make.'

'A detour?' She glanced at her watch as the driver pulled over. 'Surely we don't have time...'

'We'll be perfectly on time, I promise.' He got out of the car, rounding it and pulling open her door. She frowned up at him. *What on earth?*

'Trust me.' He offered out his hand and she took it, letting him guide her out. The driver handed him a faux fur shawl which he draped around her shoulders, but she hadn't felt the chill of winter. She'd been too preoccupied by him. Her stunning man of mystery, suave and sophisticated in his black tie...much like the night they'd first met.

'It's our one-year anniversary,' he murmured as he led her to the river, where a string quartet were playing, the ground littered with rose petals, several flickering lanterns too. The buskers were way fancier in London!

But nothing could be fancier or more beautiful than the sight of Tower Bridge lit up across the Thames. It looked just like the photograph she had on her wall back home...which of course was why he was bringing her now. Always thinking of her. Always fulfilling her dreams.

'You mean since the day we met?' she replied, her eyes drinking in the view.

'Since the day we did a lot of things,' he said low and slow and snagging her attention. 'Which is why it feels right to do this now...'

'This?'

He stepped back and her stomach fluttered. 'Tim?'

He lowered himself to the ground, his eyes never once leaving hers.

'I would have asked you months ago, but I promised you time. So here I am, one year on, Maria, down on one knee, asking you, will you be mine?'

He raised his palm, an open box with a diamond twinkled at its heart, and she gasped. The sight becoming a blur as tears filled her vision and she struggled to find her voice.

'I have Fae's blessing.'

Her eyes shot to his. 'You do?'

'For as long as I make you smile, I do, yes.'

'Her words?'

'Yes.'

'And what about Sasha?'

He smiled. 'She helped me pick out the ring.'

'In that case…' She bowed down until they were eye to eye. 'Yes, Tim! A gazillion times, yes!'

She sealed her vow with a kiss and he rose up, drawing her tight against him.

'You best put the ring on,' he murmured against her lips. 'Sasha will be looking for it as soon as we arrive.'

She eased back enough to let him take it out and then he slid it on her finger, and she felt her heart soar and settle. She was his. And he was hers.

Of all the destinations on her bucket list, she knew their journey to Happy Ever After would forever eclipse them all.

* * * * *

*If you missed the previous story in the
Sun, Sea and Swept Away miniseries,
then check out*

What Happens at the Beach...

*And if you enjoyed this story, check out these
other great reads from Rachael Stewart*

Fake Fling with the Billionaire
Unexpected Family for the Rebel Tycoon
Reluctant Bride's Baby Bombshell

All available now!